The Anatomy of Sherlock Holmes

By Don Henwood

Prologue

The train had finally come off the winding mountain track of the Swiss Alps and leveled out heading towards Germany. Inside a private berth sat Dr. John Watson. What he felt within himself was the same that was taking place just outside his window. The night was black with no lights to differentiate land from sky. Rain pelted the window leaving small streams moving across the glass. They were the tears that he refused to shed over the loss of his closest friend.

How could this have happened? One moment he was on the trail of a master criminal with Sherlock Holmes. Then, he was sent back to the village of Meiringen on what turned out to be a false medical call. Upon his return to the path towards Reichenbach Falls, the footprints he was following came to an abrupt end. What took place, and what happened there to Holmes?. The evidence was overwhelming, the outcome all too clear. But he did not want to believe it. He sat for several hours at that location hoping somehow Holmes would come walking down the trail with that ever confident expression beaming across his face. But it was not to be. Yet a ray of sunlight glinted near a crevice between rocks. Watson found Holmes' silver cigarette case lodged there. Watson opened it to find a handwritten letter from Sherlock Holmes explaining what was about to take place and further instructions if he was not to return. Was this how it would end for Sherlock Holmes? Then as the sun slipped behind the nearest peak, Dr. Watson had made his way back to the village. Where began his solo return passage home.

Watson sat alone on the train within a private berth. He kept the lights low, they were lit up only enough for him to write a few notes recording this tragedy. Where would he go from here? His life was inexplicably wrapped up with Sherlock Holmes. He knew his wife Mary would do her best to compensate, but sleuthing with Holmes had become the center of his existence.

Dr. Watson wrote, May 5th, 1891,

Without Sherlock Holmes to call upon, now I shall do my best to carry on in his too large shadow. In London, I shall continue the case we were following before leaving England. Holmes had told me just the other day that the daughter of Lord Bishop was in over her head with a suitor of questionable motives. Though this was not a typical case for Holmes to take on, he was doing it as a favor to the Lord. I make a note of this because Holmes had told me to contact a person whom at this moment I can not recount. However, there is a letter that was left on the table near Holmes' chair that has the name. My heart is troubled; therefore I do not trust myself with this information without making a note of it.

Dr. Watson turned down the light though he doubted sleep would come easily.

Chapter 1

The morning started chillier than normal for an early summer day; fog hovered low to the ground with its dew clinging to the foliage, but the sun was slowly burning it away. All signs promised that it would be another fine day in the country. In his office, Dr. Collinsworth sat at his desk reviewing a report on a patient that had resided there for a fortnight. He lifted his pen to paper and added to it.

10:00 am. June 22nd. 1892 The patients last injection was thirty six hours ago, and I expect he shall revive within the next few hours.

Above this entry was a brief history of the patients stay and cause for his having been brought to this institution. An unidentified male was brought over from a Guy's Hospital on the evening of June 8th. He was emaciated, and in a very confused state of mind. Both the constable and attending physician were unable to communicate verbally with the patient. After it was determined the doctor could be of no service, it was then at that point, he was referred to our institute.

Upon his arrival I examined him thoroughly and found him to be excessively agitated of mind. It appeared as if his brain was on overload. I also observed slight traces of scarring on his arms; I suspect some level of drug use in his past though I do not think he is just one more castoff from society.

His clothes told otherwise. From his attire one could easily tell he was a gentleman of means. Though they were slightly tattered and soiled, the fit was tailored and the fabric of quality and taste. A search of his clothing yielded little to go on. No wallet was found, only a broken pipe stem in the upper right hand interior pocket of his jacket, an empty cigarette case in the outer pocket, and a ticket stub to the continent were all he had in his possession.

I sent to Scotland Yard a detailed description of our patient and they replied that no one thus described had been reported missing. Nor has anyone responded to our inquiries with the local papers. However, I was confident he was English, and it should be only a matter of time before someone would come forward with useful information to enlighten us.

Upon his arrival and admittance, he was placed into our general ward, A. However, after three days of observation of being in the general ward, it appeared as if he was taking in all, and I mean all the stimulus going on around him. It was like a flood gate opened fully without any filters. My concern was that though he is somewhere in his mid thirties, he appeared on the verge of a major stroke even at his youthful age. So after consulting with one of my trusted colleagues, Miss Wilcox, it was decided to put him under heavy sedation until his body regained some strength. And I decided to move him into a special private room up on the third floor. So for the last ten days he has been in a drug induced sleep and fed through a tube directly into his stomach.

****

He was laying on his right side with a sheet and light weight cotton blanket covering him up to his shoulder, his unshaven face buried deep into a down feather pillow. There was rapid eye movement in his left eye, as if he was struggling to rise to the surface. Then it slowed to a stop, and the eye lid fluttered just before opening. The pillow created a white horizon in the foreground. The drugs affect had made his eyes unfocused and blurry. He blinked a few times before he saw a ray of bright natural sunlight seeping in through the heavy draped window covering and creating a long triangular beam along the wall. This was the only light that penetrated the shroud of darkness that was his room. As his mind cleared, he judged by the angle of light it must be early afternoon.

Leaden, he slowly turned onto his back, his body felt dull and heavy. It was simply much too much effort to raise his arms. So he laid there, both eyes now open, moving slowly scanning the surroundings. "Odd," he thought, perhaps his mind was playing tricks on him. He saw… He saw contours, shapes, and dimensions, but there was a lack of color, no, not a lack. It was a lack of variation of color. Looking up, the ceiling was white, the walls white, the doors and casings, white. Turning his head slightly he saw the fireplace, white. The wood box, mantle, even the match box were all white. Everything was the exact same white. His breathing became rapid, for the first time in his life; he felt the sensation of panic course through his veins. "Am I losing my mind?" Then suddenly a black streak moved across his vision. It lit upon the drapes. An inch and a half of salvation to sanity, a blowfly. With all the concentration at his disposal, he focused on it until he could make out the multi faceted eyes and distinguished the metallic blue of its body. The wings translucent, almost transparent flexed a few beats. Then the fly took wing once again. He watched the zig- zag pattern, two thirds to the left, then one third to the right, repeated over and over again. The fly had become the life line to reality.

There was a short rap on the door, and it opened giving the fly an escape to freedom. In walked a man; brown oxford shoes in need of a shine, worsted wool trousers and herringbone tweed jacket with vest, a matte black bow tie around a thick but not flabby neck. He was five eight, two hundred ten to two hundred twenty pounds. Once an athlete but gone soft with age and lack of use. He had sandy colored hair, a little graying on the side and slightly thinning on the top. His brows were thick, wild and untrimmed. The hazel eyes looking at him were from an intense person but also held the light of kindness within them. His mustache was full and covered his upper lip completely. He could see a crumb caught in the tangle of his mustache. He was an Englishman through and through.

I watched as he entered, closed the door, then took a few steps to a straight back wooden chair. He lifted it up and brought it to my bedside. As he sat, he placed a thick leather notebook in his lap; the kindness in his eyes illuminated his features. "Good afternoon." His voice was deep and clear, and thank heavens, English.

"Good afternoon," I replied in a horse whisper. My tongue felt thick and dry.

"Excellent, excellent, we are making progress." His eyes lit up with pleasure. Then he reached over to a night stand and poured water into a glass. "Here drink some of this… The medication tends to make your mouth dry."

He placed his right hand behind my head and lifted it ever so gently while placing the rim of the glass to my lips. The water was warmed to room temperature, perhaps it could have been sitting there for days, but I desired it all the same and drink eagerly. After I Finished what was in the glass, he returned it to the table and calmly sat back in his chair. Wordlessly he examined me with those penetrating eyes. Satisfied, he asked, "Now, any chance I might have your name?"

Without hesitation I replied, "Holmes, Sherlock Holmes," my voice becoming a bit clearer after quenching my thirst.

"Hello Mr. Holmes, I'm Dr. Collinsworth, and you have been our guest here for the last few weeks."

His words were like an anvil placed on my chest. My head sank deeper into my pillow, my breathing became labored. He saw from my startled expression that I was at a loss for words and confused.

"Oh, forgive me Mr. Holmes, I should have been more understanding and given you more time to come to terms with being here under these conditions."

"Where exactly am I?" Holmes asked, recovering from the initial shock.

"The Wellington Institute." Dr. Collinsworth said with kindness in his voice.

"An asylum? Sherlock questioned suspiciously.

"Well let me explain. Sixteen days ago you came to the attention of a local constable walking his beat. He found you at St. Dunstan-in-the East during the early hours just before daybreak. He said you were seated on a park bench and he observed you being rather agitated. You were talking to yourself as if you were in the presence of another person. He further determined by your tailored clothing, you were a man of means and perhaps had the misfortune of having been severely accosted on the church park grounds. According to his report, when approached you began to talk rapidly of some sort of mis-adventure, but he was unable to clearly understand where, when, and who the perpetrator was. So he thought it best to assist you to a nearby hospital and left you in their care." Here he opened his notebook to check the name. "The attending physician, a Dr. Henley, examined you for physical trauma. In his report he found some old scars, but nothing recent. He also stated that you were undernourished, but for the most part physically sound. However, he too noted your apparent state of mind and was unable to help in this area, so he sedated you with an opiate tincture." Sherlock Holmes took this in as if he were an exhausted boxer receiving unguarded body blows.

Dr. Collinsworth noticed Holmes' failing spirit. He put his hand onto Sherlock's forehead to feel his temperature, then said, "You are starting to look pale, we'll take our time with this Mr. Holmes. There is no need to rush now is there?"

It was a rare occasion for Sherlock Holmes to be at a loss for words Closing his eyes tightly trying to shut out the world that seemed in chaos he began measured breathing, a martial arts learned from his foggy past. Dr. Collinsworth reached into the breast pocket of his jacket and withdrew a capped syringe just as Holmes opened his eyes. "What's that?" he asked, though he already had a pretty good idea of what it was.

"Vitamins," he said, as he injected the serum into his patient. The doctor had lied taking on the physician's demeanor. In truth it was a sedative that took effect in a few short seconds. Holmes slipped off into a deep slumber, while Dr. Collinsworth sat there a few minutes watching him sleep, pondering who this person might be. He made brief notes of his observations of the patient. Then closed his notebook, and in his kind nature, he pulled the blanket up to Sherlock's chest and gently reached down to brush an errant shock of his hair from his face. "Sleep well Mr. Holmes, I feel we have much to discuss."

Chapter 2

Sherlock Holmes slept soundly around the clock. It was only the disturbance by the orderly's entrance that brought him back to the surface.

"Good morning sir, I have brought you some breakfast," he said brightly as he entered. A sturdy oak bed tray sat on a wheeled cart, a dome covering its contents. The orderly wheeled the cart along- side of Sherlock's bed. "Let me help you up to a sitting position." After two weeks of being bed ridden, Holmes felt weak of body. The orderly lifted him with ease placing the pillows behind his back. "Now isn't that better?" Then he picked up the bed tray and placed it in Sherlock's lap while lifting the lid from the plate. Holmes looked at the meal crestfallen and disappointed. It contained a small bowl of oatmeal with milk, a dollop of butter and a spoonful of brown sugar, a soft boiled egg, a couple slices of green apple, and a weak tea that gave off no aroma. Holmes could not remember the last time he had, sat down to a real meal and at that moment felt like he could have eaten a horse. Yet, his mouth began to water in anticipation.

"Thank you, it looks wonderful," Holmes lied.

The orderly smiled knowing full well what Holmes was really thinking, "You have not had solid food for several weeks, but we'll work up to something more substantial soon. In a few days I'll personally see to it that you'll have some of the chef's famous Cordon Bleu." Sherlock Holmes looked up at the orderly to see if he was jesting at his expense, but Holmes could tell he had a look of an honest person and took it at face value.

"After you are finished with your breakfast, I will return later to get the tray and then take you to see Dr. Collinsworth, say thirty minutes?" Holmes already had a spoonful of oatmeal in his mouth, so he simply nodded his approval. With that, the orderly made a quick departure.

Though it was for the most part a bland meal, Holmes relished it like a man soon to be on his way to the gallows. Each bite was savored, and the taste buds worked overtime. Even the weak tea, if he used his imagination, tasted somewhat like his personal favorite Earl Grey.

Not a scrap of food escaped his attention, the plate was now barren. Sherlock slid the tray down to the foot of the bed giving him room to pull off his blanket exposing a pair of thin white legs. Holmes knew some how this condition was an aberration and not his normal state of health. It was with effort he was able to swing his legs over the edge of the bed and planted his feet on the floor. The movement stirred the urgent call of nature, and would need to be dealt with very soon. He gingerly stood up hand holding onto the headboard to stabilize himself. There was a rush of coolness on his backside; he realized he was wearing one of those damnable hospital gowns that left an insurmountable gap in the back no matter how tight you tied it around yourself. This was no time to be modest, he was about to take his first tentative step as a knock was heard and the door was opened by the orderly.

"Please let me help you," the orderly said rushing to his side. It was not in Sherlock's nature to be dependent on anyone else but he knew he would have trouble crossing the room to the loo. Holmes took wobbly steps, "How much of this is drug induced and how much of it is atrophy," he asked himself. Humbled, the orderly held Sherlock by the elbow, led him to the bathroom and assisted him onto the privy.

"When you are ready, I will be just outside the door."

"Thank you,…?" Holmes said as a question.

"Clifton sir, Reggie Clifton, but everyone just calls me Reggie around here," the orderly responded.

"Thank you, Clifton," Holmes said as he stared into Reggie's face for reaction. What he received was a genuine smile as he exited the bathroom.

Reggie Clifton returned with a wheelchair and a light weight red and black checked wool blanket.

"Is that really necessary? I'm feeling better by the minute and am quite able to walk," Holmes stated with weak defiance.

"My instructions sir, are to deliver you in this chair to Dr. Collinsworth's office. What he decides after, is between the two of you," Reggie explained.

"Shouldn't I get dressed first?" Holmes was more than feeling a bit irritated with being led like a docile sheep.

"Not to worry, we can be rather informal here," Reggie replied with patience.

Holmes defiantly stood up and walked over to the wheelchair and sat. Reggie nonplussed laid the blanket over Holmes' lap and legs, and wheeled him out into the hallway. As they went down the hall, Sherlock realized this was not an ordinary asylum. The walls were papered in a fashionable style, a chair rail was freshly painted, and a sitting room at the end of the hallway was furnished with tasteful chairs and had a shelf with an abundance of titles waiting to be read. "Unusual place you have here Clifton," Holmes said over his shoulder.

"Yes, it's quite nice, and everyone seems to like it here."

"It's too soon to tell Clifton, but I would not put money on it just yet." Reggie tried his best not to laugh, but that struck him funny and he made closed mouth guffaws not missed by Sherlock Holmes.

"You were about to say something Clifton?"

"No Mr. Holmes." They traversed the remaining hallways in silence soon arriving at Dr. Collinsworth's office door. Reggie knocked softly but did not wait for an answer. He opened it and brought Holmes in. What Sherlock saw appeared more like a gentleman's den. On three sides were oiled black walnut paneled walls framing a large ornate fireplace with sculpted marble and polished brass andirons. On the opposite side was a floor to ceiling library with a host of leather bound volumes, some medical but most titles of common interest. The floor was oak, stained in a light hue with a fine hand loomed area rug from India in rich colors of reds and blues. On the area rug were two over stuffed leather chairs and sofa in a deep cocoa brown.

Dr. Collinsworth was seated at a very modest sized desk made from red cherry. He was just finishing up on putting his signature on some papers set before him as they entered.

The doctor stood and had a warm smile for Holmes. "Good morning Mr. Holmes. How are we feeling today?"

"I don't know how WE are feeling, but I'm feeling fine after a two week nap." Holmes knew he was being rude, but he didn't like the feeling of being in some other person's control.

"Yes, yes I quite understand, but it was for the best," the Doctor said.

'Who's' Holmes thought to himself as the Doctor came out from behind his desk.

"Why don't we make ourselves more comfortable," as Dr. Collinsworth pointed to the leather chairs, and then made a move to help Holmes out of the wheelchair. Holmes raised his hand in a gesture to halt him, stood on his own and moved across the room to the chair. He sat on the edge while the Doctor signaled a non verbal dismissal with his eyes to Reggie. Once seated, Dr. Collinsworth asked, "Mr. Holmes, I have some fresh tea made. Would you care to join me?"

Sherlock Holmes shook his head then asked with a hard edge to his voice, "Why am I in a nut house?"

The Doctor calmly looked at him answering, "Come now Sherlock, I may call you Sherlock, Yes?" He waited for a response but none came, only the dark eyes of a man ill at ease. "As I explained to you yesterday, you were in quite a state when the authorities asked us to access your condition and give you what care we could provide."

Holmes finally responded, "And now?" the edge softening.

"And now we need to start asking some questions," the Doctor answered.

"Am I a prisoner here or may I leave at will?" Holmes asked.

"Let us say you are our guest for the time being and your release would be mutually agreed upon." The Doctor's expression took on a fatherly look. "Please Mr. Holmes this will be much easier on both of us if you would cooperate." Holmes could see the logic to that and moved from his ridged sitting position on the edge, to sitting back into the plush cushions.

"Well in that case, a spot of tea could not hurt." Holmes felt more in control and on even ground with the Doctor. He issued a slight smile as if to say he'd not a care in the world.

After pouring the tea, Dr. Collinsworth offered Sherlock Holmes a cigar from an ornate hand carved wooden box. "They're from Cameroon, a former patient and Captain in Her Majesties Royal Army keeps me in good supply."

Though it was still mid morning, they lit their cigars and took a few minutes to enjoy them. Then Holmes held the cigar away from his mouth and studied it. A thought just beyond the veil tantalized him, but it evaporated like the smoke before his eyes, he simply could not figure it out.

"Now let us begin with telling me, what is the last memory you can recall before coming here?" the Doctor began.

Sherlock couldn't think of a reason not to cooperate, so he closed his eyes and leaned back against the cushions concentrating. It was like trying to see through a thick fog, images appeared, but too out of focus to say what they were. Finally he opened his eyes again seeing Dr. Collinsworth patiently waiting.

"I'm sorry, nothing is coming to me. It is like I know that just behind the curtain is my history but I can't find the edge to pull it back."

"Alright, then let me probe around a bit." Collinsworth rubbed his mustache with his thumb and index finger following the curve of his mouth thinking, "Can you tell me if you reside somewhere in London?"

"A good question Doctor. You asked it because I was picked up there." Holmes didn't know how he knew it but he was sure of his answer, "Yes, I do reside in London."

"If you know the location, it would help immensely," the Doctor sat forward expectantly.

Again Holmes searched from within. "No, it is not coming to me." He felt as if he was pulling on a deep root from a tree, but the memory would not yield to him.

"Let's try a different tact. How about friends?" the Doctor asked

Holmes quickly said, "I don't socialize much." Dr. Collinsworth made an imperceptible nod while writing a notation, but in the mist Holmes saw a face, "There is one, a friend, associate, colleague, I'm not sure, the name is on the tip of my tongue, West, Weston, Watson. That's it Watson."

"A first name or last? Take your time." The Doctor was getting excited.

A bead of sweat formed across Sherlock's brow and his face wrinkled. "No, no it's not there. I don't understand how this could be happening to me. Why can't I remember anything?" Frustration spilled over with each word spoken.

"On the contrary Sherlock, you did remember some things. This is just the first step in a process, like a jig saw puzzle that has many pieces. It will take time to put them together. I would like to try hypnosis with you. Perhaps we can get to your memories from a different channel." The Doctor said encouragingly.

"I consider hypnosis voodoo, I don't believe in it." Holmes looked at the Doctor questioningly.

The Doctor gave a belly laugh that broke the tension, "Then you have nothing to lose by letting me try, now do you?"

"No, you're right, eliminate all other possibilities to find the right answer." Holmes took a last draw on his cigar before extinguishing it in the ashtray nearby.

"I think perhaps we should stop at this point and begin again later this afternoon. In the meantime we will ask Reggie to make inquiries to locate this Watson through the usual channels.

"Doctor, do you suppose I could have something to wear besides this hospital gown? I feel rather exposed." He lifted the edges of his gown with both hands and waved them slightly.

The Doctor laughed again at Holmes' dry sense of humor. Then the Doctor turned serious again, "Will you promise me you won't wander away if I accommodate you?"

"You have my word as a gentleman," Sherlock smiled for the first time.

"Fine, then I will ask Reggie to find something appropriate and have them brought to your room." Dr. Collinsworth rose in a fluid motion and walked over to his desk. There he pushed a button from the underside of the desk and within moments Reggie Clifton entered through the door.

"Reggie, Mr. Holmes would like to take a walk in our lovely gardens this morning. Would you please find suitable attire for him to wear?"

"Yes Doctor, I think I can find something in his size, though it might not be up to date in style. Then again no one seems to mind around here all that much anyway. Come Mr. Holmes, your chariot awaits you." Reggie Clifton wheeled the wheelchair over to where Holmes was sitting and stood by, "When your ready sir, I will return you to your room."

In the hallway heading back to his room, Holmes commented, "It did not take you very long after Dr. Collinsworth buzzed for you. You were sitting just outside in the hall." Holmes turned his head upward to see Clifton's reaction.

"Yes Mr. Holmes, it is for Dr. Collinsworth's safety with new patients, one never knows how these first meetings will go, and he prefers the private setting whenever possible."

Holmes retorted, "Do I have the sort of look to be dangerous?"

"Mr. Holmes, I am much more than just an orderly. It is part of my duties to assess each patient's potential for violence, and take appropriate measures. And, in answer to your question, yes I do consider you as potentially dangerous."

"That would explain why a Royal Dragoon in his prime would be transporting me in this chair."

"But how do you know this Mr. Holmes?" Clifton asked surprised.

"The dragon tattoo on you right arm. Some men chose to identify themselves that way between regiments, and yours is from The First Royal Dragoons."

Reggie Clifton smiled and gave a little chuckle, "Very observant Mr. Holmes. It only confirms my opinion that you could very well be dangerous."

****

Sherlock Holmes did not have to wait long for the clothes promised. Reggie came back to his room within twenty minutes. "I hope these will do for now sir. It's hard to find a suit for someone of your height." Reggie Clifton laid them on the bed and left Holmes to dress in peace.

Sherlock returned to the bathroom to douse his face with cold water. The shock of it invigorated him and he felt more alert than before. 'Whose face was that staring back at him'. He combed his thick ebony hair with his hand thinking, that he could not believe he would ever let his hair grow to this length, and was there a decent barber here? At least someone had kept his face occasionally shaved while he had been drugged. No matter he could deal with all that later.

He returned to his bedside and picked up the charcoal hued tweed pants and pulled them on, they were the right length but a size too large though not enough to worry about. Next a stiffly starched white shirt was put on, feeling rather reassuring and civilized. The coat was even larger and hung loosely from his frame. He felt the material between his thumb and index finger, this was quality fabric, tailored in one of London's finest establishments along Savile Row. He wasn't sure how he could possibly know this, but he did.

****

Holmes walked through the hall undisturbed, down a set of winding stairs and out through the south entrance. He blinked from a sun not often seen like this in England, a near cloudless sky and warmer temperatures than usual, it was an invitation for a gentleman to stroll. Across the drive Sherlock saw a pea rock walkway through a boxwood hedge. He entered into a proper manicured English garden. His body felt stiff from lack of use, his ill fitting clothes hung loosely as he moved along. He wondered for a moment who's clothing he wore and where he was at this moment. Was some poor soul locked away in a padded room babbling away with incoherent thoughts never to see a day as such as this, and would he also end up in that same place?

What Holmes did know was whoever wore these, smoked Cuban cigars. He could detect the faintest hint of aroma that lingered on the jacket, but other aromas vied for his attention. The scent of Daphne and Lilacs and Clematis all mingled together with the soft breeze.

The pathway arced to the right in an ever diminishing curve until he reached a well attended rose garden. At it's center was a white trellis gazebo with rose vines inter weaved over many years. The roses, crimson red as blood stood out against the stark white wood. Inside a white wicker bench stood sentry, a thick cushioned seat invited a sojourner to take respite. Holmes heeded the call and climbed the two short steps and sat down. Here he closed his eyes and emptied his mind of all the clutter.

Concentrating on sounds near, he heard a bumble bee droning from flower to flower. Then a flicker off to the left ten feet up a trunk, pecking the bark in search of his meal. Mentally reaching out further, the faint but distance sound of a heavy wagon wheel turning and the distinct clop of a work horse hoof in a steady rhythm on a well trod path. Holmes' brow furrowed with effort. Then he opened his eyes concluding the institute was devoid of the buzz and commotion of city life and therefore was situated in the countryside. It would be these kind of exorcises of the mind that would yield answers as to how and why he had come to be in this place.

Chapter 3

On the stroke of 4 pm, Holmes was ushered into Dr. Collinsworth's office. The hunter green drapes were drawn closed, lighting was soft, and a flickering amber danced across the dark paneling from a welcoming fire in the fireplace. Holmes immediately noticed it was a log-less fire. He moved closer to examine the source.

"Marvelous isn't it?" Collinsworth said as he backed his chair away from the desk and rose with a sense of grace. "A resident here crafted it for me. He's a genius in many ways, too bad he has an insatiability appetite for murder." A slight curl at the edge of his mouth betrayed an aborted smile.

Sherlock looked at the doctor inquisitively but asked no further question. Instead, he moved over to one of the leather chairs and slid it soundlessly across the area rug nearer the fireplace. Then sat down with his feet just shy of touching the andirons, with a relaxed posture, almost a slouch, and a faint smile at the edge of his lips. The good Doctor understood the challenge Holmes was presenting and knew he had thrown down the gauntlet.

In response, the Doctor said, "Let's keep this informal shall we?" Then he turned his back to Holmes and took a few steps to a built-in cabinet. Which upon opening revealed a quite nicely stocked liquor cabinet. Collinsworth poured two snifters of brandy. The aromatic scent quickly filled the room and the dark amber liquid coated the glass with its film as the doctor reached out handing one to Sherlock.

"Are you trying to make me forget that I'm a prisoner in an asylum?" The fire light danced off of Holmes' eyes.

Collinsworth began laughing until it started to make himself cough, "Really Mr. Holmes." Still chuckling he set his glass on the mantle and pulled the other chair over by the fireplace directly across from Holmes. Retrieving his brandy, he took his seat and wordlessly sat waiting for Holmes to speak. Sherlock sat with his drink held close to his lips, taking a sip, the warm liquid filled his senses with pleasure, and his eyes twinkled over the rim of the glass as he measured the countenance of the man across from him.

"Now, isn't this better?" The doctor lifted his glass, "To your health." Each man measured the other in the silence.

The doctor waited a minute or two letting the brandy do its magic, "Mr. Holmes, may I call you Sherlock, less formal that way."

"And do I still call you Dr. Collinsworth or just doctor?" A bit of sarcasm in his tone of voice.

"My Christian name is Reginald, but my friends call me Reggie and I would be most comfortable if you would consider me just that."

"Well Reggie, I think I would prefer Holmes if it's all the same to you. And by the way, is it not confusing to your patients that both you and your associate are Reggie's?"

"Here we refer to him as Clifton; it saves confusion." To bring the conversation back to the reason for being here in the first place, The doctor leaned back into his seat and began by asking,"Can you recall any memory?"

Sherlock mimicked the doctor sinking deeper into his seat before speaking. He was resigned to the fact of his circumstances. "I remember when I was a child, someone called me Gayle or Gay."

"Someone close to you?" The doctor's ears perked up.

"I don't know, but I think I didn't want to be called that in school. Boys look for anything to tease one another. I can remember a few fights with much bigger students who called me a sissy."

"Can you recall the school?"

Holmes concentrated a moment, "I don't know, I can picture the building, ivy covered and in need of maintenance."

"How old were you then?"

"I'm not sure, five maybe six years old. I can remember the boys I fought with were at least twice my age."

"Well, I'll do my best not to provoke you. I have a feeling I would regret it deeply." Holmes smiled at the Doctor's jest.

"Why is it I can recall memories like this but have no clue who I am?" Holmes asked.

"Think of the brain like layers or rings on a tree trunk. Early events are closest to the core, deeply embedded and like a clean slate the first memories have a deeper impact on your development; therefore they are more prone to recall. Some things tend to leave more of an impression, friends, family, or important events. But it is not consistent, I have had patients tell me in detail memories of their first Christmas and the toys they received, but couldn't tell me where they were last week. I believe, every thing you have seen or done is imprinted in your brain, some we can recall with almost infinite clarity, and others a clouded image.

Together, we will," the   doctor said with great compassion, "work on peeling back those layers, probing bits and pieces until we have a complete picture."

"So hypnosis is going to do all that?" Holmes asked skeptically.

"No it is only one tool, but effective as I hope you will see. The real work will be as you recall strands of information, I will ask questions that should over time, help complete the picture. With more memories come other thoughts, stone upon stone we will build back your past."

"How long do you think this will take?" Holmes questioned.

"I only wish I knew the answer to that question. It could be days, months, maybe years. I do not want to promise a cure, Mr. Holmes. There is a chance that what ever trauma you experienced will prevent you from ever really knowing who you are, even if we find out from other sources what have been your life details."

"Then it is possible I could be here for the rest of my life, a shell of whom I am, never to know my past entirely." Holmes shoulders visibly sagged as he asked the question.

"Please don't be discouraged, I only wanted to be honest with you. Give it some time and trust me to delve into your past. This is what I do, and others have had great success. This home is a wonderful place, and you could do much worse out in the world. I firmly believe even if we don't experience a full recovery, you now have full faculty of your senses and would be able to function outside of this facility."

Dr. Collinsworth leaned back into his seat and finished his drink in a single gulp. "With your permission Mr. Holmes, I would like to try the hypnosis on you now and see what comes from it."

"I don't think it will work on me."

"Then we have nothing to lose by trying, now do we?" He gave Holmes his warmest smile and moved to the front of his chair lifting his right hand a few feet in front of him, index finger raised.

Holmes sat straighter in his seat, put his brandy glass on the floor, and inhaled then exhaled deeply.

"Holmes, concentrate on my finger. Eliminate everything else from view, hear only my voice." Holmes' eyes narrowed while focusing on the tip of the finger, seeing the swirls on the skin unique to Dr. Collinsworth. The Doctor's voice became softer as he spoke,"Let your body relax. Sink into the cushions; they are a soft and protective cloud." His voice became mesmerizing. "You feel comforted, peaceful, time stands still. Let the feeling of sleep envelop you; your eyes are growing heavy, you can't keep them open." Holmes' eyes slowly sank with only a flutter of protest.

His breathing moved slow and steady. "You will continue to hear my voice as you go deeper. Go back Sherlock, back in time. A time that is clear to you."

The Doctor waited a minute in silence. "What do you see, Sherlock?"

He spoke barely above a whisper,"There is room, with bars, no, a crib. I see through the bars of a crib. I'm alone, I have been alone for a long time."

The doctor asked, "What are you feeling right now?"

"I feel as if I have been abandoned there, desperate! Where is my mother? Why won't she come get me?" Sherlock's eyes moved rapidly behind his eye lids, as he took in air in gulps.

"I'm here with you Sherlock, you are not alone now, tell me what see." The Doctor's voice was reassuring.

"Everything. I see everything. I know the number of beats my heart makes in a minute. If I could have spoken, I could have told you the thread count on the sheet that covered me."

"Being in this room, alone, does this happen often?" The doctor leaned forward in his chair to catch every word spoken.

"Every day, it is my whole life. To survive, I take in my surroundings. No detail misses my attention. Knowledge,

knowledge means life." Sherlock's body had become rigid, his hands in a tight fist turning white as the blood was squeezed out.

"Sherlock, I want you to come back now. You feel rested. Your body is relaxing again. When I touch your shoulder, you will wake." He reached out and touched him lightly. Holmes' eyes fluttered briefly, then opened slowly. He took a deep breath and let it out through his mouth.

"So, did it happen Reggie?" Holmes said slightly sarcastic before retrieving his drink from the floor.

"Quite well in fact, surely you recall at least some of what you said to me."

Holmes studied him for a moment, "Not a word. I assumed the warm fire and brandy caused me to nod off for just a moment."

Dr. Collinsworth stood up taking his empty glass in hand, "Well, Rome wasn't built in a day, but we are off to a good start." Pausing, "can I freshen that drink?"

Sherlock handed the glass to the Doctor, and moments later the two of them were staring into the fire. After several minutes of quiet reflection, the Doctor said, to no one in particular, "Dinner is at six." Then he was again quiet for awhile. He looked to Holmes and said, "You might find it interesting to join us tonight. The staff and residents dine together in the main floor dining room. Perhaps I will see you then." He rose and went to his desk as Holmes left the office unescorted.

The Doctor sat down and pulled a file out from the top drawer with Sherlock Holmes written on the cover. With a pencil he made an entry; Mr. Holmes subjected himself to hypnosis, and while under, he recalled a very early childhood memory, perhaps only slightly older than an infant. It was remarkable what he said, and he appears to have a fascinating intellect, an ability to take in his surroundings much like a photograph. No even that is an inadequate description, it is well beyond that. No detail seems to escape him. It is too early to say for sure, but I suspect he is an orphan and one that was not particularly well cared for. To compensate, he has developed the skills and ability to be totally self-aware. However, he was not able to recall anything he had said to me, and that concerns me greatly. At this early stage, I would have to take an educated guess that whatever trauma that has occurred in his recent past could very well be overwhelmingly blocking him from his memories.

Chapter 4

Sherlock descended the last flight of stairs down a sweeping half circle into the main foyer, the ceiling done in hand sculptured plaster, faces of Greek gods stared down from twenty feet above. A salt and pepper marble wainscot, level with the upper reaches of the door casings surrounded the room and electric wall sconces spaced evenly gave off a soft amber glow. Leather over stuffed chairs and love seats placed nearby and dark wood side tables with the latest edition of The Times invited one to linger. In the center of the room, a round reception desk containing a cut glass vase with a profusion of bright colored flowers anchored the space. The entrance to the dining room was to the left. French double doors with a white lace curtain stood open to the guests.

He slowly walked over feeling a little uncomfortable, and his ill fitting clothes didn't help when he saw just how opulent the setting, with white linen tablecloth, crystal glassware and sterling silver serving trays. It was no less appointed than any fine gentleman's club. The white silk ceiling to floor drapes partially covered the well-maintained window trim painted in a high gloss.

The floor gleamed spotlessly and reflected back the subtle grain of the teak wood. Even the crystal chandelier that sent radiant light across the ceiling spoke of money. His attire this evening was completely unacceptable in his opinion. He scanned for the most out of the way table hoping to disappear into the background. Having been an early arrival he made his way to a table over in the far corner next to the window that looked out onto the grounds facing east, and from it, one could see the comings and goings of both the dining room and the world outside.

The residents and staff filtered in by ones and twos talking in low voices but with moments of banter and laughter interspersed. It seemed to Holmes so out of place for an asylum. It simply did not fit his image of such a facility or what he thought it should have been, but how would he know anyway? Had he been confined to one before? Not knowing was maddening. What he was sure of, was that many of these diners had been residing here for quite some time. A family atmosphere prevailed, with seats taken by virtue of who they were talking to at that moment.

Then a man caught Sherlock's eye, as he came through the double entry doors. He was in his early thirties, stocky, but still showing the contours of muscle that had grown softer with lack of use. He stood at the entrance looking directly at Holmes, with a hint of a sinister smile moving briefly across his face. Then a stone cold expression of hatred took hold, and just as quickly a practiced jovial smile and an air of nonchalance masked his demeanor. As Holmes watched him, he weaved his way through the slalom of crowded tables and came to Sherlock's table.

Standing just to the left of Holmes in front of the next seat he asked,"May I?" Sherlock nodded his assent, but from somewhere within him a sense of alarm coursed through his veins.

The man sank heavily into the well-cushioned chair,"I'm surprised to see you here."

"Sir?" Holmes said with a furrowed brow.

"My name is Anthony Colton," he spoke as if he were expecting some particular response.

Holmes innocently responded, "I'm Sherlock Holmes," extending his right hand.

Colton leaned back into his chair not bothering to accept Holmes' hand,"Yes you are," he said with a new look of pleasure.

Holmes was confused, "Should I know you?... Forgive me I'm not quite myself at the moment. Perhaps if you would remind me of our acquaintance?"

"No, no please forgive me, I am not good at social graces, "He took Holmes' hand that still was extended though it had dropped below half-mast. Colton's grip was like a vice testing Sherlock's resolve. Then without warning, Anthony stood up,"If you will excuse me, I find that I'm not particularly hungry this evening." He walked away before Sherlock could respond.

Holmes thought to himself, "What an odd encounter." Sherlock was thinking about what had just taken place when Dr. Collinsworth strolled into the dining room stopping at a few tables exchanging greetings with the residents. His smile warm and genuine. A comforting hand laid upon a shoulder or two like from the Bishop of Canterbury at High Mass. Slowly he made his way through the room until he came to Sherlock's table."If you are not tired of me, I would like to join you this evening." The Doctor's countenance was disarming.

Holmes appeared momentarily distracted, "By all means Dr. Collinsworth. Oh, right, or do you still insist on a first name basis?" Holmes could not help himself. The issue of first or last names was still unresolved. The Doctor pulled out a chair from across the table and sighed as he lowered his body into it as if he had been digging ditches all day. Holmes asked, "Tough day at the office?" still with the edge of sarcasm.

The Doctor reached out and took a deep draught of water from a glass set in front of him before responding with a faint smile, "Knowing about the lives led here, or in some cases not knowing, can be a bit trying at times." His gaze turned from the residences to Sherlock," and how are you feeling this evening?" The sting in the comment was well aimed.

"Is this our next session, a doctor always on duty?" The frost was thick, Holmes not giving an inch.

Collinsworth's expression conveyed almost a fatherly demeanor, "No my friend, it's just that at times after hypnosis, one is prone to have difficulty getting their bearings straight, and sometimes thoughts or memories will suddenly flood into the light. I have seen it often enough." He watched Holmes for any reaction.

"Tell me about Anthony Colton," Holmes spoke with an edge to his voice.

"Anthony? You know Anthony Colton?" The doctor could not hide his surprise.

"I made his acquaintance earlier. He came up to my table, introduced himself, and almost as if he had some critical engagement he had forgotten, Colton excused himself and left saying, he was not the sociable type. I find that rather curious behavior. So, are you on a first name basis with him?" giving the doctor the third degree.

Collinsworth pondered a moment, "Anthony Colton goes out of his way to avoid interaction with any of the residents here. So, when he says he is not sociable, that would be an understatement. I do, however, find it very interesting that he sought you out in particular. Any idea as to why he would pick you out from all who are dining here tonight?"

Holmes delayed his answer seeing the server rolling a small cart towards them. Two domed plates and a bottle of red wine rode silently across the floor, steam escaping from under the rim. The musky aroma wafted as the lids were removed. Baron of Beef, pearl onions, boiled red and white potatoes, and asparagus were artfully displayed. And a small bowl containing Yorkshire pudding fresh from the oven, aromatically mixed together to arouse the palate. The server placed the meals before them and poured a glass of dark red Merlot into the crystal glassware before returning to the kitchen.

Holmes could not hide his amazement, "Do you always eat this well?" He picked up his silverware and sliced into the moist beef, mouth watering in anticipation. With that first bite, he closed his eyes in delight chewing slowly, allowing the flavor to fill his senses fully.

Then, Dr. Collinsworth raised his glass and said, "A toast to Bacchus, the god of wine and mirth."

Holmes lifted his glass and took a sip of the wine rolling it across his tongue. A satisfied expression said more than words could have.

"We are a private facility and very well funded at that. I must say, it's one of the perks that keeps me here and as you can see, it is starting to show on me as well." Collinsworth made a gesture of pulling on his belt to make his point.

They slipped into a comfortable silence each quietly enjoying their meal. It was not until they both had finished and Holmes was finishing the last sip of his glass of wine that the Doctor asked again, "I'm still waiting to hear your thoughts as to why Anthony Colton spoke with you."

Holmes chose not to share his feelings of alarm with meeting Colton, so his answer was short and direct." None whatsoever."

"Well then I'll save that question for him when we next meet," the Doctor said with eyebrows furrowed.

Holmes could tell the good Doctor was not believing his sparse response. So he began to stand and exit before Collinsworth could press the question. "If you will excuse me, I think I'll take a constitution in the garden before I retire."

"Then good evening Mr. Holmes," he paused only a moment before adding, "shall we meet again in my office say ten a.m.?"

Sherlock gave him a genuine smile and said,"I haven't any other appointments scheduled tomorrow, so I don't see why not. Until then, good night."

Doctor Collinsworth watched Holmes exit the dining room thinking this man was an enigma that would not soon to be resolved.

Chapter 5

Sherlock Holmes slept well considering his encounter with Anthony Colton. He was simply not bothered by these minor details in life, though at this moment he couldn't tell you why that was true. Holmes laid in bed with his hands propping up the pillow, strangely wishing he had a pipe available to smoke. That was a sensation he had not felt for quite some time. From the corner of his eye, he noticed the wardrobe closet door was barely ajar. He knew he had not left it that way last night. He had undressed and left his clothing laid across the back of the chair near his bed. Though that was out of character, the events of the day and a heavy meal had taken a toll on him. He was surprised at himself for not having noticed before when he had returned to his room last night. And because he was still feeling the effects of having been drugged for so long, he allowed himself grace, considering his state of mind.

Rising from his bed, Holmes proceeded to the closet and opened the doors. Inside was the welcomed sight of five suits of slight variation, not Tailor made, but high quality off the rack styles. A half dozen starched white shirts, neatly folded, and an equal number of under shirts and pants laid in an open drawer.

Sherlock washed up and dressed in his new clothing, the fit almost to perfection. Reggie Clifton must have been the one to pick out the clothing, and he would need to thank him next time their paths crossed. Holmes looked at himself in the mirror, a crease formed across his brow, eyes stared deeply into his reflection. "What are you doing here Holmes?" he asked aloud. Intuitively he knew he was one who was always in control of his surrounding. Holmes put a forced smile on his face in an attempt to shake the very feeling of being out of control. He straightened his tie one last time and went downstairs to the dining room for tea and scones.

Sherlock Holmes descended the stairs feeling much more comfortable than the night before. Fresh new clothes made him feel like a new man ready to meet the day head on. Sunlight streamed through the windows casting moving shadows across the foyer, and dust motes drifted aimlessly with the slightest disturbance of motion from any passersby. Holmes entered the dining room finding Reggie Clifton loading a plate with a mountain of food. Sherlock walked up behind him and laid a hand on Reggie's shoulder and said, "So are you keeping a platoon hidden somewhere?"

Clifton wheeled around with a plate in hand. A slice of bacon slid off onto to the floor, Reggie had an embarrassed look on his face, "Oh, good morning Mr. Holmes." He looked down at his plate and then sheepishly grinned at Sherlock, "I don't always get a chance to eat three squares a day, so I tend to load up when I can."

"You are the one who filled my closet yesterday?" Clifton nodded affirmation. "Thank you, the suits fit well." Holmes would have extended his hand except for the plate held in Reggie's two hands.

"You're welcome, sir. I was the person who attended your needs when you were incapacitated, so it was rather easy to pick out the right size when the time came. I hope you approve of my choices, Dr. Collinsworth is utterly helpless when it comes to making this kind of decision."

"Quite the contrary, you could be a valet for nobility. I approve of your taste and style most heartily."

"You do me a great honor sir." He spoke as he gave a slight bow at the shoulders, "but If you will excuse me, I have much to do this morning. Good day." With that Clifton left Holmes to order his breakfast.

Sherlock Holmes proceeded back to the same table at which he had sat the night before. The sunlight dissected the linen-clothed table equally. He sat with his back to the wall which gave him a clear view of the entire dining room. For some reason, this seating arrangement felt most natural. A young woman came up to his table asking what he would like this morning. Her face fresh and eyes bright, she wore no makeup, and her was hair pinned in a bun. It was evident to Holmes that she was working here by choice doing something she wanted to do, not one who felt she had no options in life. This place continued to surprise him and challenged his ideas of what a place like this was supposed to be. He asked for Earl Grey tea and scones if they had them.

"I believe they are just coming out of the oven as we speak. The Chef is particularly proud of his recipe, something he brought back with him when he trained in Paris." She smiled warmly and left Holmes to his thoughts.

Within a few minutes, she returned with a tray carrying a teapot covered with a tea cozy and a small platter of scones with butter, jams, and jellies to apply as desired. Wordlessly she set the table, poured the first cup and left with the same charming smile. Sherlock picked up a scone. It was almost too hot to hold in his hand. When he broke it open, a cloud of steam burst forth. He applied strawberry jam with a small table knife and unceremoniously bite it in half and the second half disappeared just as quickly. His appetite was returning with a vengeance.

The tea he poured back into the pot, then first adding milk to his cup, he poured back the tea and added a small scoop of sugar. He stirred his cup for ten seconds without thinking about it. It occurred to him that this was a ritual he had done his entire life. Then lifting the cup to his lips, he took in the aromatic scent of the Earl Grey tea, earthy and English to the core. This tea brought balance to the world to an Englishman's heart; all things could be endured as long as he had this elixir.

As Holmes was finishing his breakfast, Anthony Colton entered the room. Colton made straight away to the counter where a coffee urn sat. He poured a cup and exited the room without looking in either direction, indifferent to his surroundings. That same small alarm set off within Holmes giving him resolve to pursue further questioning with Dr. Collinsworth.

****

Holmes arrived precisely on the stroke of ten. Knocking twice on the office door, Dr. Collinsworth opened it with a pleasant countenance on his face."Good morning Sherlock, how did you sleep?"

Sherlock ignored the question of sleeping but said,"Fine Reggie." Each word was spoken with cold sarcasm. Sherlock Holmes was not comfortable with a first name basis. He felt like it was just not part of his makeup. "I'm sorry Doctor, but calling you Reggie somehow doesn't fit with me. I have always been most comfortable with using last names. So if it's all the same with you, I would prefer being called Holmes, and you, Dr. Collinsworth."

"Outstanding Mr. Holmes. A clear memory has surfaced, and by all means feel free to call me anything you like, just not a charlatan." The doctor chuckled at his joke and clapped Holmes on the back as he ushered him further into his office. Leading him still with his hand firmly placed on Holmes' back he guided him over to the overstuffed chairs. "Can I get you anything, tea, coffee? It's a bit early for anything stronger even here, though it's five o'clock somewhere in the world." The Doctor was obviously in a good mood.

"An answer" Holmes was direct as ever.

"And that is?" The Doctor, quickly focusing in on the question.

"I need you to tell me about Anthony Colton."

The Doctor could see Holmes was most serious in his question, and that his encounter with Anthony Colton deeply disturbed him, "Yes," the Doctor paused a moment thinking what to say or not to say. "Well, Anthony has resided here for the last five years give or take a month or so. He comes from a very wealthy and powerful family. Normally he would be in a different facility than this but for his family influence."

Holmes broke in," He's the one who designed this fireplace."
He stated that with utter confidence.

"Well yes, that's correct," the Doctor agreed.

Holmes further stated," And the facility you're speaking of
would be an asylum for the criminally insane."

"Again you are right. Let me try to explain. Reggie Clifton
was initially hired specifically to watch over Anthony. We were
very concerned for the safety of our other residents. However,
over time Anthony proved to be quite docile and kept to himself.
We have had no problems with his stay here. In fact, he seems to
be completely adjusted to his daily routines, and though I can't
say specifically, he has made significant progress in his treatment.
So, with that Reggie's duties have been directed in other areas and
now assists me with a broader range of tasks. That being said,
why the interest in him Mr. Holmes? It can't only be your chance
encounter with him last night. I saw it in your eyes when I asked
you about it. Please, something is bothering you about him and
telling me might help."

Holmes raised his hand to his face and rubbed both cheeks
simultaneously with thumb and fingers giving him a moment to
formulate his thoughts, "I'm not sure, I get the feeling that
Anthony Colton and I have crossed paths before." Sherlock stared
at the ceiling trying to dig deeper into the sensation.

"Interesting, can you tell me why you feel that way. Perhaps you had business dealings with him, or is it that you feel threatened by him?"

Holmes said matter of factually, "No, not threatened, alarmed. I don't know. I don't know any more than an impression."

"Let's leave it at that for now, and we can revisit it at another time. If you recall any thoughts or images later, come, see me day or night, I'm here to help. Speaking of which, I would like to try hypnotizing you again and see what comes up."

"All right, but I have one more question before we proceed. The clothes in my closet, you anticipate an extended stay?" Holmes said it as both a statement and a question.

"As I have said before Mr. Holmes, sometimes this process takes time. Bits and pieces put together like a stone mason building from the ground up. At first, it looks like chaos, but as he moves forward, a building takes shape. In your case, something might trigger a memory, a face or an arrangement of a room. Even a smell could cause a flash of remembrance, sometimes small, other times wholes blocks of memory could flood in. We just don't know what will be the one thing that will remove the veil before your eyes. The mind is a very complicated machine and needs to be handled delicately."

Dr. Collinsworth assumed the position as he had the day before, hand held out, index finger extended leading Holmes into a calm state. As Sherlock went deeper under his influence, the Doctor said in his steady voice, "Go back Sherlock, go back to a time when you felt peaceful and happy." Collinsworth waited while Holmes sat stock still. Several minutes passed silently, before Holmes began to speak, "There is no peace." Collinsworth waited, "There is, motion."

"Where are you, Sherlock?"

Holmes' voice rose,"I'm in a gymnasium, a vast area covered with floor mats in the center of the room. There are dozens of boys with me listening to an instructor. I'm standing before him, separate from the other students. The instructor is looking directly at me, speaking to me, but not to me. I'm being chastised for hurting another boy, but he doesn't know that several of the boys had attacked me."

The doctor asked, "How did it happen?"

Holmes took a deep breath and exhaled slowly reliving the moment. "The instructor had left the room, three boys older than myself saw an opportunity to get at me. My back was turned from them, and I was talking with a new boy who had just arrived. I was being tackled from behind, then knocked to the floor. When I shed the boy from me by turning over onto my back, one of the other boys was standing over me, with his right foot raised and ready to stomp on my chest. I grabbed his foot with both hands and twisted it to the right, then struck him at the knee cap using my left knee driving it upward while continuing to twist his leg to the right. He collapsed to the floor like a fallen tree and wailed bloody murder. My blow was measured, held back from what I could have done. He would have a deep bone bruise instead of my dislocating his knee joint. I showed mercy, where had he had the chance; he would have delighted in cracking my ribs." Sherlock's breath remained steady as Collinsworth noted that the recounting of this episode was not making Holmes feel agitated. Holmes continued, "The loud wailing brought the instructor running back in to see what was going on. The other two boys immediately pointed their fingers at me saying that I had gone after their friend. Then the instructor told the two boys to help the injured boy to be taken to his office. By then the rest of the boys in the room had gathered where we stood and waited to see what would happen.

The instructor waited for the three boys to leave before turning to me. He spoke not really to me, but more to the class, "Holmes I understand those boys are bullies, and they are not the only ones, but you are responsible for avoiding these confrontations if possible. Your skills are far superior to theirs. Do you understand me?" I did understand him. He was giving fair warning to any other boy that I was not one to pick on just because I was much younger than they were."

Collinsworth asked, "How old were you?"

"Twelve."

"And the boys that attacked you?"

"Sixteen, seventeen, maybe."

"How are you feeling at this moment?"

Holmes said, "Proud, confident, independent."

Dr. Collinsworth wanted to go deeper,"Sherlock, I want you to go to a time later in life. You feel relaxed; you are in control of what you see and feel. Tell me, where are you now?"

The pages turn ahead in the book of Holmes, his body posture was erect, eyes closed, but no tension showed on his face. Slowly a wisp of a smile appeared before he spoke, "I'm, in a gallery... A half circle of seats, thirty-two rows rising above a podium. They are filled with students. I'm at a university, and the professor is writing a formula on the chalkboard, but I can hardly sit still in my seat because he is wrong. He is explaining the potency of Dumb Cane on the human anatomy. He is underestimating its use and effect." Sherlock's voice rose as he recounted this.

"Why are you so agitated about this?" The Doctor was intrigued by Sherlock's ardor.

"Because he and I have clashed on multiple occasions. He, like so many at the universities, refuse to move into the modern age. Old thoughts, old ways. Why can't they plainly see what is of course new science? We choose to be blinded by tradition." Holmes then became quiet as if a cloud had enveloped him.

Dr. Collinsworth perceived that no more would come from this session. "Sherlock, you will wake now, quite refreshed. You will remember what has been spoken here today. I will count down from five when I reach one you will open your eyes and tell me what you have said under hypnosis. Five, four, three, two, one." Sherlock's eyes fluttered; briefly, he took a long slow breath and let it out with a sigh. "How do you feel Holmes?"

"I feel as if I have been asleep for hours." His feet turned up with the heels firmly planted to earth, and his back was slightly arching making his point.

"Please tell me what you remember?" Dr. Collinsworth asked.

Holmes' brow furrowed, "I'm sorry, but I don't recall anything spoken between us. I only remember your voice speaking as if from the far end of a tunnel before falling asleep."

Dr. Collinsworth rose and stepped over to the fireplace placing his left hand on the mantle and slid his right hand into his coat pocket. Collinsworth looked perplexed but remained silent. Sherlock sat motionlessly watching the doctor for some reaction.

The only sound came from the subtle hiss of gas being fed into the fireplace. Finally, Dr. Collinsworth looked at Holmes, as a frown appeared and he let out a breath through his nose that wheezed like a tea kettle on boil. "Curious..." Pausing another moment, "I have not encountered this before. Though you gave me information in depth and you could follow my suggestions without deviations, you seem completely blocked from retaining the shared memory. Always before in my dealings with hypnosis, I have been able to elicit a cognitive response, and if not all, then most of what was said. The patient would be able to remember what they had spoken under hypnosis. But in your case, not even the remotest detail was retained. Frankly, I'm stumped, Mr. Holmes. I can only theorize that perhaps there is some profound and traumatic experience that your sub-conscience is unwilling or unable to deal with." Dr. Collinsworth then looked kindly at Holmes, "Take heart, Mr. Holmes, we have just started the process, and we will get to the bottom of this yet, I promise. In the meantime, I'll make inquiries to see if there is a connection between you and Anthony Colton. Perhaps this will shed some light on this mystery. Shall we meet again this time tomorrow?" Sherlock vacated his seat, shook hands with the doctor and exited the room knowing he would have to analyze the situation further.

Chapter 6

Holmes left Dr. Collinsworth's office wandering the halls aimlessly. Why had he failed to recall any of his memories during hypnosis? He knew instinctively his mind did not work that way. He could recount every detail of his room. He could describe without fault the layout of the dining room, the position of the tables and placement of the chairs. He could, if asked, tell where each resident sat the night before, so this drawing a blank was disconcerning on so many levels. It was only now that the magnitude of his lost memory hit him. Just how long has this been going on? Had he been roaming the streets for days or had it been years? He had no reference point from which to measure. Perhaps if his old clothes were available, he could deduce a timeline from them. He would have to ask Clifton where his clothing were being kept. Then there is the question of Anthony Colton. Holmes knew without a doubt that Colton knew who he, Sherlock Holmes was, and therefore, it was imperative that he find out all he could about him in return.

It was time to go directly to the source, Anthony Colton had to be somewhere on the grounds. Holmes was confident that Colton was not one who would keep to his room all day. Colton was a caged lion, claws retracted but the danger ever present. He may fool the doctor and Reggie Clifton with his docile lifestyle here. But Holmes had seen the look in Colton's eyes the other night. Murder laid just under the surface. A ticking time bomb waiting for the right opportunity. For whatever reasons, this man had been able to manipulate himself into being here and not locked away in a prison cell. This was another piece of the puzzle that Holmes would have to put together.

Sherlock descended the last set of stairs and exited the building through a side door. He went through the gardens first hoping to find Colton in a place of privacy. It would be convenient to speak with him without distractions. However, the gardens were empty but for bees and birds. Holmes then headed back to the building and went around the corner to the south side. On this side of the building was the veranda. It occupied the entire length of the building. It extended out twelve feet of tongue and groove ceiling with Corinthian style columns and white balustrade rails. Teak tables and chairs at random placings had residences dressed in summer wear drinking tea or lemonade in dewy tumblers, a scene right of a George Seurat painting. Holmes didn't expect to see Anthony Colton here among so many people, but to his surprise, Colton in truth was sitting at a table near the far end. Sitting with him was Dr. Collinsworth, leaning over a chess board, deep in thought.

As Sherlock climbed the last few steps, he could see the progression of the ongoing match, Collinsworth was in trouble. Anthony Colton was only three moves from checkmate.

"Holmes," Colton called out as if greeting an old friend. Sherlock approached the table putting on an air of nonchalance, his face unreadable. Collinsworth had not moved a muscle, his concentration focused on the game board and had not registered Colton's greeting. It was not until Sherlock stood beside the table that Dr. Collinsworth jolted slightly at the pair of legs now in view. When he realized that the legs belonged to Sherlock, he sighed deeply and said, "Hello Mr. Holmes, have you come to watch me fall upon my sword yet again?"

"A good general knows when to surrender," Holmes replied, giving little in the way of condolences.

"I don't know why I continue to put myself through this misery; this is about as far as I ever get in a match with him. You know, I always thought of myself as a player, that is until we started this humbling slaughter five years ago. But to this day, I think just one more game, one unexpected move and the result would favor me. Just once, Holmes, that's all I ask, just one glorious match where I can sit back and gloat like he is doing at this very moment."

And it was true, Anthony Colton was doing exactly what the Doctor said. He was sitting back with his arms crossed and with a smirk plastered on his face. He looked up at Sherlock with cold and calculating eyes saying, "Perhaps we should do battle, Mr. Holmes." From the inflection of his voice, Sherlock knew that he meant something much more than a simple game of chess.

Holmes locked eyes with him giving back an equal challenge. Dr. Collinsworth perceived that something was amiss and though he had made a few subtle inquiries, he had yet to get any answers as to how or if there were any connections between these two men. "Perhaps you would like to take my chair, Holmes. It's time I go off and lick my wounds." Then the doctor heaved his solid frame upward with surprising grace. "Good luck Holmes, you're going to need it. Anthony." He said in salutation as he walked away leaving the two combatants still staring at each other.

Holmes lowered himself into the seat that radiated warmth left over from the last heated battle, "Then the game is afoot." Holmes began to replace the pieces on his side of the board.

Colton flashed a Cheshire cat smile, the one who had just eaten the canary. "Yes Mr. Holmes, it certainly has." He sat forward and put together his side of the board. Then while still leaning over the board he said, "Shall we begin Holmes?"

The layered meaning was quite evident, but Sherlock played innocent and kept his expression neutral. Anthony made the first move on the board and Holmes countered within seconds. The pace of the game was frantic, and no stop clock was needed. On Sherlock's ninth move, he moved his King's Bishop as a defensive counter. Colton suddenly slowed on his next play, but Holmes attacked with his Queen charging forward. "Checkmate Colton."

Anthony Colton had not seen it coming. Anger, almost hatred, flashed across his face. Holmes said calmly, "You approached the game too confidently Colton without knowing your opponent."

Colton tried to regain his composure as he said, "I won't make that mistake next time." The words dripped with contempt, his left eye twitched as he suddenly rose and spoke softly, "Until we meet again." Then he walked away, his body language speaking volumes.

Holmes followed Anthony from a discreet distance leading into the dining room, where Colton poured himself a cup of tea but did not raise it to his lips. He stood stock still staring at the cup in his hand, then without warning, he threw the cup and contents against the wall, tea bled down leaving a stain in its path. Colton, with his back to anyone who might have witnessed his display, straightened his jacket, fiddled with his tie and calmly exited as if nothing had happened.

Chapter 7

Sherlock had been standing at the far end of the foyer watching Anthony Colton's outburst. For some reason, it gave him a deep satisfaction to have gotten under his skin. He also realized there was danger following this course of action, but he felt that Colton was the link to his recovery. Holmes stood there analyzing what he had observed over the last twenty minutes. Was Colton's fury directly caused by a sudden and unexpected loss at chess? He thought not. The look in Colton's eye was maniacal. For a brief moment, Holmes almost anticipated an attack, with Anthony leaping over the table going for his throat. Holmes had reflexively prepared for such a response as he had felt his body instinctively shift into a balance that would give him the advantage had Colton advanced.

There was the fact that Anthony Colton could go from barely containing his rage, to in the blink of an eye, a seemingly composed demeanor. Then only to moments later letting the rage out unobserved, the fury expressing itself. It was time to seek out information from Reggie Clifton, the man who had been initially assigned to watch over this insane murderer.

Sherlock walked over to the reception desk in the center of the foyer. A woman dressed in a nurse's uniform sat with her back to him. Holmes casually leaned over the desk with his elbow anchored on the counter and his hand holding his chin with his thumb and index finger giving the appearance of nonchalance. For Holmes had no idea if this nurse knew if he was a patient here or not. "Excuse me, can you please direct me to where I might find Mr. Clifton's office?"

The nurse was holding a clipboard in her hand at the time. She finished notating something on it and then turned towards him, a warm smile greeted Holmes. "He has an office on the second floor, room two-twelve. Can I have someone show you the way?"

"Thank you, that will not be necessary. "Holmes returned the smile in a functionary way.

He made to move away from the desk as she said, "You will need to sign in before you go upstairs." She opened a register and waited.

"My name is Sherlock Holmes."

"Thank you." Her smile became even more radiant; her long lashes batted languorously.

Sherlock's eyes widen slightly, my God, is she's flirting with me? He thought. Strangely, his hands started to feel clammy, and a hint of shortness of breath overtook him. He almost stuttered with his reply, "You're so kind," then extricated himself as quickly as possible. He headed to the foot of the winding stairs and took them two at a time. Meanwhile, the nurse watched him ascending, knowing full well who Sherlock Holmes was.

As he reached the second floor, he paused to collect himself. Why had it been so unnerving to have a young lady flirt with him? Without realizing it, he was reconstructing the moment of meeting her. The image was crowding in upon him. An elegant crown of auburn hair, shiny to the point of glistening. Her eyes, a gray-green, the color of a storming sea. Fair, creamy skin without blemish or flaw. A delicate slightly upturned nose, befitting her features. Her lips, streamlined and soft, inviting, like rose petals, and the color she wore reminded him of a pale version of the night owl rose. Her high cheek bone and petite chin completed a… Yes, an angelic face.

His thinking came to a crashing halt. "Get hold of yourself, Holmes," he mumbled aloud. These thoughts somehow felt foreign to him, a lack of self-control, but, stimulating none the less. Sherlock put them away for a later time to examine these impressions when he could view them more objectively.

Midway down the hall was room two-twelve on the right-hand side, a small brass nameplate at eye level had Reggie Clifton's name on it. Sherlock knocked twice lightly. From within a voice called out, "Come in." Holmes opened the door and entered into a smallish office, space adorned with a simple dark oak desk with only a telephone sitting on the surface. Two Burgundy Queen Anne chairs, a teak wood file cabinet, and a fine hand woven area rug covered a portion of the dark stained v-g fir floor, all simple but tasteful.

"Why Mr. Holmes, what a pleasant surprise to see you. Please come in; you're most welcome." Reggie stood in greeting and shook Sherlock's hand, then gestured for him to sit. As Sherlock took his seat, Reggie asked, "What can I do for you, Mr. Holmes?"

"Your rug, from Amritsar India, it is quite beautiful," Sherlock studied it for a moment longer.

"Yes it is, isn't it? A memento from my days in the service. I'm sure however you didn't come here to talk rugs," Reggie then waited patiently.

"No, but I do love to take whatever time necessary to appreciate an object of beauty," Holmes paused momentarily, "what can you tell me about Anthony Colton?" It was like a bolt of lightning striking from the sky.

Sherlock received a similar response as from Dr. Collinsworth. "You know him?" a heightened level of concern strained his voice. "Please be careful Mr. Holmes when it comes to any interaction with Anthony Colton. He may well be a resident here, but he is without a doubt, in my opinion, a very dangerous man."

"Then why is he not locked up in some dark hole with the key thrown away? I know from Dr. Collinsworth that his family is wealthy and apparently has a strong influence."

Reggie Clifton leaned forward in his chair in a posture of sharing a confidence. He gave Holmes an appraising look before saying, "I really shouldn't be telling you this, and would appreciate your complete discretion on what I'm about to reveal. Anthony Colton is a nephew to the Queen. And because of that, certain accommodations were arranged. Mr. Holmes, this facility, and its operations are funded by the Royal Family, and because of that, we are able to help many people who might not get this level of care otherwise. So if you will please tell me why you are asking about him?"

Sherlock weighed his options and decided to be straightforward with Reggie Clifton. He relayed to him how Anthony Colton had introduced himself at dinner the night before and then about running across him again earlier this morning while playing chess with Dr. Collinsworth. Sherlock chose, for the moment to leave out some of the other details.

Reggie smiled knowingly, "Mr. Holmes, I already know he spoke with you last night. And, you left out beating him at chess a short while ago. I'm not the only person here assigned to keep an eye on him." Reggie's eyes narrowed in on Sherlock, "Keep your distance from him, Mr. Holmes." The last statement said not as a suggestion but as a command.

Sherlock said, "Well, I won't take any more of your time. You have been most helpful, thank you." Both men rose, and Reggie again extended his hand. As they shook, Clifton's hand squeezed like a vise making sure Holmes understood his meaning

Chapter 8

Sherlock Holmes left Clifton's office quite intrigued. There was much to Anthony Colton he had yet to discover, and this somehow felt normal to him, like hounds on the chase. The information Reggie Clifton gave him was a fascinating piece of the puzzle. He stood just outside of the office door contemplating his next move. What came to him was an over whelming desire for a smoke, a pipe to be exact. It was like a light had been turned on. Up until this moment, he had not given it a moments thought. He asked himself, "had he always been a smoker, or is this desire part of a ritual stimulated by what was occurring at this time?" Holmes smiled at himself for the first time since his awakening. He felt good, alive, a challenge to his wit, this would be more than a distraction from his issue of a lost memory. He may not know who he is or if he ever will know, but for now, the blood was running warm and he was in pursuit.

As Sherlock retraced his path and went back to the reception desk on the main floor, as he was observed by the nurse at the station, and she noted the new spring in his step. When he went up to her she smiled with both her eyes and her rosy lips, "Hello again Mr. Holmes, is there anything else I can do for you?" Her expression and body language invited a more intimate level of conversation. Sherlock was drawn into the liquid depth of her eyes mildly shocked with himself for being captivated with this young women.

"As a matter of fact, you may be of great service to me. I'm in need of a new pipe and tobacco."

The nurse was surprised by the statement, surely Holmes' request was not just a sudden need to partake in a gentleman's pastime, but she remained passive, "Why of course, we do have a commissary right down the hall on this level. If you go all the way down to the end, it will be on your left. I'm sure they will have every thing you need." Then she coyly asked, "Will you be returning anytime soon to visit us?" She was most curious to see what his response would be.

A flash of embarrassment crossed his face, but he leaned in and in a conspirator's voice said, "If you must know, I'm a guest here for a short while."

The nurse visibly brightened, "Well that's wonderful Mr. Holmes, I suppose we will have an opportunity to see each other yet again." Holmes caught the possible double meaning to her words and felt unexpectedly both flattered and pleased.

Before he could change his mind, he said, "I will look forward to it too... Miss?"

"Wilcox, Fiona Wilcox." Her smile beamed radiantly like a fresh summer day.

Sherlock nodded an acknowledgment and returned a subdued smile, "Until then Miss Wilcox." Holmes then exited down the hall as she kept her eyes on his retreat thinking that there is much more to this man than meets the eye. She and Dr. Collinsworth would have much to discuss later.

****

Sherlock entered the commissary to find shelves well stocked with a wide variety of goods for every possible need, from toiletries to books. Ties, ascots, and hats, and yes a delightful display of pipes in all sizes, shapes, and colors. There were also multiple brands of tobacco from around the world. He felt like a kid in a candy store as he pondered over his selection. Holmes picked up several different styles of pipes getting a feel for how they felt in his hand, while each time was viewing himself in a small mirror hanging on the wall. Having chosen the one that felt right, he perused his options of tobacco. After looking over all the exotic blends, Holmes instead chose common black shag in a simple tin container for no apparent reason that he could think of, it just felt right. He took his selection to the counter and laid them on the glass case. The clerk immediately greeted Holmes, "Is there anything else you need sir?"

"I'm not sure if this is possible, but I'm staying here and do not have the funds available at this moment to purchase these items. However..."

Before Sherlock could finish his statement, the clerk spoke up, "It is not a problem at all sir, we are here for your convenience. What ever your needs are, we can help, and if you do not see it, we will do our best to have that item ordered and brought here as soon as possible." The shopkeeper gave that universal look of pride that one has when they feel they have everything at their disposal and have anticipated before hand the need of the customer.

"Thank you, and there is just one more small item I need, matches."

The clerk smiled and stooped a bit to reach under the counter pulling out a small silver container, "Will this do?" He handed the little box to Holmes.

Sherlock scrutinized it, first feeling the raised pattern then looking close up at the artistic hand hammered ivy pattern that wrapped around the box. "This is quite beautiful I must say."

"Yes, it is, one of our residents here was a silversmith and likes to keep his hand in it. Dr. Collinsworth feels that doing so helps keep him calm and gives himself a sense of peace that otherwise he might not feel."

Sherlock was taken aback by that statement. "Tell me if I'm correct. Is it my understanding that Dr. Collinsworth shares his diagnosis of his patients with all the staff?"

The clerk chuckled quietly, "sir, the residents and staff here see themselves more as a family. We try to learn how to meet the needs and preferences of each person here. The staff is given necessary information according to the level in which they serve the residents. I assure you, this facility is run with the utmost professional standards." He then glanced at the match box and said, "When you need a refill of matches, please come back, and I'll take care of it for you."

Holmes caught the drift that the clerk was not going to answer any more questions. "You're most kind, thank you." Sherlock left with his new cache to find a quiet place in which to have a smoke and ponder the facts he now had.

Through the front doors and into the garden Holmes found himself drawn back to the Gazebo. He had yet to come across another person in the garden, so it gave him a sense of refuge. He sat on the bench and filled the bowl of the pipe. Striking a match, he took several quick short draws on the stem, then drew a deep draft into his lungs. He held it momentarily then exhaled, the smoke blowing out the match. A second draw, letting the taste linger in his mouth, gave him the sensation that this was not new to him though it had been quite some time since he had last imbibed.

Holmes turned his thoughts to the task at hand and weighed the facts as he saw them, Anthony Colton had freedom of movement, but there were many eyes on him. He was also "The Golden Goose," this facility and it's running was funded by Royalty and with that strong influence dictated how Colton was treated. Holmes instinctively knew Anthony Colton was one who was biding his time here, and would act out when it suited his desires. Was Sherlock the only one to see this, or did the staff realize they walked a fine line between the daily peaceful operations and potential disaster?

Without consciously thinking about her, Fiona Wilcox crept into his thoughts. "Yes, she is a beautiful woman, he thought," but there is much more to her. He could see it in her eyes, intelligence well above her station. Her questions had layers of meaning beyond the words. Why did Holmes feel that way? He simply had to trust his instincts. Then a disturbing thought occurred to him. Was he married? Was there a Mrs. Holmes out there who thought she was a widow? No, that just didn't seem right to Sherlock, but he looked at his left hand for any evidence of having had a ring on it in the past. Somehow Sherlock Holmes felt that women have not played a significant role in his life. Then as if he was looking into the thickest of London fogs, he could almost sense that there was an older woman who did something for him. The fog in his mind though was too thick. Try as he might, he could not get a hold of the thought. No matter, that glimpse gave Holmes some encouragement. A small but elusive memory had come to mind, and on that, he could build upon.

Later that evening Sherlock entered the dining room, and as was becoming a habit, he went to the same table by the window. Once seated, an attendant came to his table and said, "Good evening sir, tonight we are serving a seafood dish I think you will quite enjoy, and may I recommend this Chablis? I believe that it would complement your dinner very well."

Holmes responded distractedly, "Yes please, that would be fine," while watching the room. In the recesses of his mind, who was he looking for? Was it Anthony Colton, or Fiona Wilcox? The mere thought of that deeply troubled him, but why?

Then, appearing as if on cue, Fiona Wilcox entered through the French doors. Her hair that had been loose earlier was now tied up in a bun accenting her delicate facial features. Nurse Wilcox was no longer wearing her nurse's uniform. Instead, she wore a long silk dress crimson red with a bold black sash looped around her slender waist. She scanned the room as if looking for something or someone. Her eyes turned to Sherlock, and then her face lit up. She came towards him walking only as a woman can, all eyes in the room were trained on her. Sherlock could tell she was enjoying the moment.

"Why Mr. Holmes, what a pleasant surprise," she said demurely.

Sherlock had two conflicting thoughts going through him at the same time. First, he wasn't sure how comfortable he was with her having sought him out, and second what was this electrical sensation running through his body. Okay, he had to admit, he was slightly intrigued by her presence and attention. Sherlock was ingrained with being a gentleman. So, with an extended hand presenting the table, he said, "It would be my pleasure if you would join me for dinner." Five empty chairs remained at his table, she chose the one right next to him and glided into the seat with grace.

"In truth Mr. Holmes, I'm not a shy girl. I waited until I saw you come in here and was planning all along to sit with you. I also wanted to make a grand entrance. So, how did I do?" Her smile was entirely enchanting.

Holmes returned her smile saying, "A member of the Royal Family could not have garnered more attention than your regal entrance."

"I'm delighted then." She reached over and put her right hand upon Holmes' hand ever so delicately.

His first response was his hand flinched but almost unnoticeable to the touch. He had caught himself due to an over riding sensation. What was it? Pleasure? What ever it was, it felt foreign and strange. Again his memory loss left him at a disadvantage. So why does this woman cause such a stir in me, and why do I feel so off kilter in her presence? He thought. Sherlock was at a loss for words like a youth at his first school function, and it showed on his face.

"Do I make you that uncomfortable?" Her eyes narrowed, "You look like a cat caught in an ally with a pack of dogs at its heels." She tried to give comfort with a caring expression.

Holmes realized this was no ordinary woman. There was a depth to her, insightful, intuitive, and intelligent. There were layers to her faculties yet to be uncovered and analyzed. Sherlock picked up the carafe and poured her a glass of wine giving himself time to collect his thoughts. Up until this moment, she had the upper hand. Sherlock chose his words to turn the tide in his favor, "Do you often dine with the loonies here?" He watched closely for her reaction.

Fiona burst out laughing, catching Holmes by surprise. "You are wicked Mr. Holmes, and no, I spoke with Dr. Collinsworth earlier this afternoon just checking to be sure that you were not as you like to say, a nut case. He assured me you were quite safe."

Holmes' body language relaxed a bit, "In that case, if I'm about to have a psychotic event, I'll do my best to let you know in advance." He then sat back in his chair feeling a verbal victory was won.

She shook her head slowly saying, "Wicked, wicked, wicked."

The rest of the evening passed in pleasant conversation with an enchanting and elegant woman over a supper of Lobster Thermidor, Caesar salad, and lightly sauteed vegetables. All the while Sherlock Holmes observed Anthony Colton making casual passes by the entrance door with an ever increasing look of malice on his face.

Chapter 9

The next morning Sherlock Holmes arrived at Dr. Collinsworth's office feeling refreshed and uplifted from last night's dinner with nurse Wilcox. The appointment was scheduled for ten, and he was there at the door as the clock was striking the hour from within. Knowing he was expected, he entered without the formality of knocking. As the day was already warm, the Doctor had drawn back the drapes and opened the French doors letting in the fresh and warm air. "Good morning Mr. Holmes," Dr. Collinsworth glanced at his pocket watch even though the grandfather clock had just finished chiming. "Right on time as usual. I could set my watch by your timing. Can you tell me, is this typical or not?"

Sherlock thought for a moment before saying, "I don't think so, but then I don't have all that much to distract me, and in truth, I am rather starting to enjoy these little visits."

"My, my, my, you seem to be in a jolly mood. Perhaps we should sit outside on the balcony today. After all, we don't get this nice of weather all that often."

As Sherlock approached, Dr. Collinsworth extended his right arm and clasped Holmes around his shoulder while leading him over the threshold. Outside there was a black wrought iron table and two teak chairs the same as the ones on the veranda on the south side of the building. The only difference was, these had thick padded cushions tied in place. "Have a seat, Mr. Holmes, I'll be right back."

Sherlock sat down facing the gardens beyond. The very gardens he thought he had exclusive privacy too. Had he been observed by Dr. Collinsworth, and did it really matter anyway. As he thought these things, the sun shone upon him, warming his skin. He squinted his eyes at half mast until they could adjust to the brightness. Shortly the doctor returned with a tray containing an ice-filled pitcher with an amber liquid. Tea? Sherlock speculated. He had never had tea in any other form than piping hot. Collinsworth set the small tray on the table, sunlight created prisms of light angling across the tray. The mix of hot sun and ice in the tea caused the pitcher to form a haze with droplets of moisture sliding down and pooling at the base.

The doctor saw Sherlock's curious expression and said, "Something I picked up in India. It was always too bloody hot to drink tea in a civilized way, so one had to adapt to one's surroundings." He poured the tea for Sherlock into a crystal tumbler, "A couple spoonfuls of sugar and I think you will be pleasantly surprised how good this can be."

Sherlock did as suggested, stirring in the sugar then taking a sip. He thought to himself, "This has to be an acquired taste," but nodded approvingly in spite of what his opinion of the taste really was. "Well?" Collinsworth asked.

Sherlock did not want to lie, so he simply said, "Um mm." This brought a pleased smile to the Doctors face.

"I thought that perhaps we would just talk today, no hypnosis." The Doctor sat in the other chair and took a deep draught of his drink, wiping his mouth afterward with a linen napkin.

Holmes had been gazing at the gardens while the Doctor had spoken to him. "And what is it you want to talk about?" Then, Holmes turned in his chair to face the doctor.

Dr. Collinsworth's expression turned serious, and he looked as if what he was about to say was practiced ahead of time, "Frankly, in all my years of using hypnosis in therapy, I have never had a patient not be able to recall what was said during a session. I've experienced times of partial blocks, mostly small details, but yours seems a total block. That is unless you are not completely honest with me. Are you, Mr. Holmes?"

Sherlock was quick to answer, "Please, believe me, I want to find out how I came to be here in this condition just as much as you do. I will be truthful with you, and if anything comes to mind or memory is triggered, I will let you know promptly." Holmes quickly added, "I may not remember my past, but I feel my instincts are as sharp as ever, and because of that I'm sure that Anthony Colton knows me. The fact that I can not remember what I say in hypnosis, that, I'll leave to you. My instincts also tell me you are an excellent doctor and I have complete confidence in your abilities to get to the bottom of this."

The Doctor leaned over the table for emphasis, man to man, "From what you have said while under hypnosis, I believe you are a remarkable man with an incredible ability to disseminate information both visually and cognitively. That being said, I will do my best to dig deeper to find any connection between you and Anthony Colton, short of just asking him since he wouldn't tell me if he did."

Holmes matched the Doctor's posture, "There is one more question I would ask you. Last night I had an unexpected dinner companion, Fiona Wilcox." The Doctor interrupted him, "Our desk nurse."

"Yes, she sought me out at dinner making quite a splash doing so." The doctor could not keep back a smile, "You are certainly right about that, I heard from several people about her entrance and her gorgeous red silk dress. I'm only sorry I missed it."

Holmes looked more intensely at him, "I could not very well brush her off with all eyes on us, but I'm concerned she might have put herself in danger by doing so."

The Doctor became slightly alarmed, "And why is that?"

Sherlock said the words that could have put an arrow through Dr. Collinsworth's heart, "Anthony Colton observed us dining together, and for whatever reasons, he did not look too pleased."

"Okay Mr. Holmes, I will let Clifton know to keep an eye out to see if Anthony shows any interest in Miss Wilcox. I'm sure though, he is just being himself." Then it dawned on him, "Is Miss Wilcox the reason you are in such a good mood?"

Sherlock, perhaps for the first time in his life felt embarrassed. He had tried to put last evening and the strange feelings aside but to no avail. Collinsworth was just too good at his job, he saw through him and asked the very question Holmes couldn't bring himself to ask. "I have to admit, Miss Wilcox is most charming, but for whatever reasons she tried desperately to act less intelligent than she really is. Why do you suppose doctor?"

Dr. Collinsworth took on the look of a proud father, "You would not believe the half of it, Mr. Holmes. She is one of the most intelligent women I have had the pleasure to know. She, in fact, has two books on the subject of cognitive study that have turned the world of psychology on its head, though she had to use a male pen name to publish them. Unfortunately, it is a man's world where women are thought of as the weaker sex, and therefore, incapable of such talent, more the pity. I for years have tried to encourage her to continue her education, even offered to pay the full costs through the Foundation here. She would make a magnificent doctor in her own right, a man's world or not. Yet each time I have offered, she says she is quite happy with where she is and what she does. Fiona always looks me in the eyes and states she would not have it any other way." Then a mischievous smile came upon the Doctor, "You know Mr. Holmes, to my knowledge she has never shown the least interest in anyone who has ever come through these doors, whether patient or staff." The Doctor lifted the ice tea to his lips but hesitated to drink, "If I were you, I would do whatever it took to keep her interest. I guarantee you, sir, you could not possibly do better than someone of her caliber, why If I were twenty years younger..." The Doctor's expression took on a far off look as his voice faded into silence.

Sherlock waited patiently for the Doctor to recover from his reverie. He picked up his iced tea glass getting his hand wet from the condensation and taking another sip. No, he thought, this was not a taste he would be interested in developing. Returning the glass to the table, Holmes held out his wet palm contemplating the physics of condensation before rubbing his hands together to dry them. The motion brought back the Doctors attention, "I'm sorry Mr. Holmes, I was lost in thought there for a moment."

"That's quite all right Doctor, Watson often said the same about me."

Collinsworth was suddenly alert, "Excuse me, Watson?" The Doctor, focusing in on Sherlock, "you said that name on the first day we spoke. Is there something you now remember?"

Holmes took a moment and looked at his hands reconstructing his thought pattern, "Watson could never sit still. He would pace the room from one end to the other all the while haranguing me to get up out of my chair and go half cocked off to..." His voice trailed into silence. His expression turning dark and clouded.

"Off to where Holmes?" Collinsworth asked excitedly.

The dark clouds suddenly turned into a violent storm, anger in his voice, "I don't know," he shouted. Sherlock was surprised with himself. Anger is the loss of self-control, and self-control was his mantra. That thought sprung up like a geyser from deep within. Yes, Holmes realized self-control was an integral part of his makeup, a core value, but why? Even to him, it seemed rigid and limiting. As Sherlock thought these thoughts, Dr. Collinsworth sat still, his demeanor calm and benign. "I'm sorry Dr. Collinsworth, that was rude of me to shout at you like that," his emotions now completely reigned in.

"Quite the contrary Holmes, don't you see, you had a breakthrough, and I'm most pleased?" The doctor relaxed back into his seat and looked out past Sherlock collecting his thoughts. "Let's try this, close your eyes, block out all distractions, and just concentrate on that name. Let it sink in and take root. Don't force any thoughts, let it gently come from within." Sherlock closed his eyes. "Now take a few deep breaths, hold them briefly and let them out slowly." Holmes complied. "Again." The doctor could physically see Sherlock calming, hands laid open in his lap, his chest rising and falling rhythmically.

Sherlock spoke softly as if from a dream, "Watson is a doctor." Then silence again.

Collinsworth asked in the same quiet voice, "Medical or psychiatric?" The Doctor speculated whether this might not be the first time Holmes had been in an asylum. The answer rolled from Holmes' lips quickly, "Medical." Then a moment's pause, "that's it, that's all I can tell you. I can almost see his face in my mind's eye, but so out of focus."

Sherlock opened his eyes to a beaming smile from the Doctor. "Good show, good show Holmes. Now we not only have a name, we now know that this person is a doctor. That, my friend, will narrow down our search significantly. Who knows, with any luck at all, we could find him within a few days. I will get Reggie on this right away. Yes, yes, outstanding, Mr. Holmes." Dr. Collinsworth's enthusiasm was barely contained. Then a devilish look came upon the Doctor. "Shall we celebrate Holmes, perhaps a nip of cognac? It's five o'clock somewhere in the world, and besides, I can tell I haven't made a convert of you with iced tea."

The Doctor rose and crossed the threshold before Holmes could either accept or decline. Sherlock was still contemplating what had just transpired. He felt physically drained, his body melted into the chair. The synapses in his brain fired sluggishly, Sherlock was in a stupor.

The Doctor returned with two snifters containing about an ounce of cognac in each. He handed one to Sherlock and raised his to his nose taking in a deep breath reveling in the rich aroma, allowing the moment of pleasure to his senses. Then he said to Sherlock, "This is the elixir of the Gods, to your health Sherlock." The Doctor threw back the drink all at once while Holmes remained motionless. "Go ahead Holmes, it will do you good." Sherlock complied mechanically allowing the liquid to revive his spirits. Then the Doctor laid a hand on Sherlock's shoulder and said, "Let's give it a couple days rest before our next appointment. Give yourself a chance to catch up with this new information. Sometimes when a person has a major breakthrough other memories will come to light spontaneously. Try to relax Holmes, let yourself heal without forcing it. Maybe another walk in the garden would help, I find that it helps me with sorting my thoughts." Sherlock looked into a set of eyes that held great compassion.

After Holmes had left, Dr. Collinsworth called for Reggie Clifton. "Reggie, see if we can find a Doctor Watson. I don't know if it's a first or last name, but Mr. Holmes prefers using last names so I would probably assume last. He may be living or dead, real or fiction, but do your best. And Reggie, let me know if Anthony Colton starts to show any interest in Fiona. Mr. Holmes seems to think she could be in some sort of danger with him. On this, I think I'll trust Sherlock's instinct. He has deduced much already about Anthony, and that makes me nervous."

Reggie had a stern look saying, "I told Sherlock to keep his distance from Anthony. The last thing we need is for him to kill the golden goose."

"Please Reggie, just do as I ask let me worry about Sherlock Holmes."

Chapter 10

Sherlock took Dr. Collinsworth's suggestion and meandered out into the garden. Instead of taking the path that led to the gazebo, he passed on to a trail through a small grove of Japanese Maples. The Doctor had said not to let the lack of memory bother him, time was an ally. This allowed Holmes to be in this space with a new sense of peace and strangely he was enjoying being out on the grounds. Passing through the grove, Sherlock found the perimeter of the estate, an off white stucco wall six feet tall with random clumps of grass in need of attention, and round portals spaced evenly went in both directions. This wall was not particularly secure, one could have easily scaled over using the few oak trees that ran along the grounds with thick branches reaching over to the other side. Even as a child, he could have made his escape with ease. No, this wall was ornamental at best. Had other patients climbed over on occasion, or others entered this way as opposed to the front gate. Then again, why would anybody in their right mind do that? Sherlock smiled inwardly at his own joke. Then he thought again about the patients here, why would they choose to leave a velvet prison. They had everything they needed here and not a care in the world. That led Holmes to the next thought, Anthony Colton. What kept him here? Holmes was sure Colton could care less about this place. It was a mere convenience, a place to bide his time. Anthony Colton was a time bomb just waiting to go off leaving a trail of death and destruction in his path. From what Sherlock picked up from Colton, he felt he was a prime candidate for that angst. So what would keep me from shimmying up the nearest tree and wandering off? Holmes was sure he could now handle himself just fine out in the world. While these thoughts had floated through his mind, he had unconsciously moved over to the nearby tree. A thick knot made for a natural step, he placed his foot on it and stepped up grabbing a large branch. He pulled himself up and stood on the branch. Only a few feet out and he could jump to freedom. He took the first step, the second step, then stopped in mid stride. Miss Wilcox popped into his mind, vulnerable and unaware of the potential hazard she could face. Holmes could not even begin to entertain the thought of a personal interest in her. Somehow he sensed that he had always remained aloof when it came to the fairer sex, not that he could not appreciate their presence, Sherlock felt that perhaps he couldn't be bothered with their womanly ways. He could not see himself having someone fuss over him. These were only impressions, but strong ones at that. "Here I am standing on the edge of freedom, yet unwilling to leave because of a woman," he thought. The conflict held him in place. He suddenly burst out laughing,"Every question has an answer," Sherlock said out loud. He climbed back down, gracefully jumping the last few feet. He looked around to see if he had been seen, straightened his jacket and dusted off a bit of detritus. Then resumed his garden walk saying to himself, "I'm not staying for any other reason than to protect her." That settled, he could put aside any uncomfortable speculation for now concerning him and Miss Wilcox.

Holmes returned to his room and refreshed himself, then changed clothing before going downstairs for dinner. At the bottom of the stairs, Sherlock checked his tie, looking into a small mirror that hung on the wall, a mirror placed there for this very purpose, one more subtle convenience provided by the staff. He stood at the entrance of the dining room. The warm weather seemed to have invigorated the residents. Many tables set with dinner ware on the off-white linen cloth seated chatting groups of residents. The walls echoed the cacophony of voices blending into a soft drone, indistinguishable, but not offensive.

Before he felt it, he sensed a presence just to his right. An arm slid through his right arm, his defensive instincts almost took over, but he held them in check. "Well, good evening Sherlock," Fiona said with a radiant smile.

Holmes remained outwardly calm saying, "Good evening to you Miss Wilcox. By your gesture, I take it that we are dining together again." He appraised her attire, Tonight she was dressed in a black satin gown that accentuated her creamy white skin. Her hair was unencumbered, almost wild. The modest plunge of the neckline framed a small silver cross that drew attention whether intended or not to her shapely figure. Fiona wore a perfume that reminded Holmes of the Mignonette, a flower that gave off the fragrance of vanilla-raspberry. On the hand that had slipped through Sherlock's arm, was a wine colored garnet ring on her index finger, several smaller stones surrounding a larger stone in the center. All this he had observed in a second or two with a quick glance, natural as breathing, but somehow disturbing none the less.

Together they crossed the room arm in arm, while heads turned in their direction, Sherlock could easily see why. Fiona Wilcox was a beautiful woman, she moved with grace and made eye contact with residents naturally, her smile was genuine and inviting. This attention was contrary to how Holmes would prefer. He would rather blend into his environment, observe, but not be observed. It put him at a disadvantage if he could not remain anonymous, yet he adjusted to his part and played the courtier.

Sherlock's usual table was occupied, so they took one in the far corner away from the window. He pulled out the chair for Miss Wilcox, seated her, then sat in a seat with his back to the wall giving him a clear view of the rest of the dining room. The patrons now returned to their conversations as if Holmes and nurse Wilcox had never passed through. This was absolutely fine by Holmes. He surveyed the room, barely moving his eyes, then noticed that Miss Wilcox was looking at him expectantly. A very awkward moment hung in the air, she was waiting for him to start the conversation. The night before Holmes was more at ease, but now it was different. What did he have to say to this woman, watch your back? No, that was no way to begin a conversation. He was trusting the Doctor and Reggie Clifton to do their job and keep a close eye on Colton. She turned slightly, and the light reflected off her silver cross. Sherlock felt a flood of relief, "That is a lovely cross you are wearing tonight." Holmes reached for the water glass conveying a casualness he did not feel.

She fingered the cross with her left hand tracing the lines,"My mother gave this to me on my sixteenth birthday. She told me it was made from the mines in the Holy Land." She smiled impishly, "At least that's what the merchant had told her."

In spite of himself, Sherlock was beginning to be captivated by her facial features as she spoke. He noticed a charming twitch on her right cheek from saying any word that started with the letter 'M,' and there was an enchanting light and life that shone brightly in her eyes. Fiona Wilcox exuded a level of confidence that came from being bright, happy, and well-adjusted. The latter two

Holmes doubted about himself. Sherlock needed to change this line of thought, "Dr. Collinsworth regards you highly."

"The feeling is mutual. The Doctor is a brilliant man and is considered one of the best in his field. I am privileged to be working with one such as he." She paused momentarily then said,"Now Sherlock, enough of him. Let's talk about you."

Holmes had no idea if or how much Dr. Collinsworth had told Miss Wilcox about him. So he chose to keep it neutral. In his most charming manner, he said, "If only I could. The reason I'm here is that I don't know who I am." He said it in a way that tried to convey humor or "truly it's no big deal." His half smile inviting her to join in on the joke.

She lit up at the challenge, "Well let's look at this logically. I can tell you are a gentleman, cultured, and most certainly intelligent," she appraised him with her eyes,"handsome, in a rugged sort of way," her eyes twinkled as she spoke. With each word, Holmes turned a bit redder. A general praising he could handle but to have a woman say he was handsome. That was altogether a different sensation.

She saw that she might have taken it a bit far, and made Sherlock feel uncomfortable. So she quickly changed tact. "According to Dr. Collinsworth, he says you are very astute with your surroundings. He told me you seem able to take in details that most everyone else might miss." Her expression took on the look of a child in a candy store. She commanded, "Close your eyes." He complied. "It would be too easy if I asked you, what I am wearing. So, tell me how many people are sitting at the table three tables to your right. And tell me what they are wearing tonight."

Holmes smiled at the game. "Four diners, two men, two women. Both men are wearing pure Irish linen suits. The one nearest the kitchen door has on a straw hat with a red band and a feather from the tail of a Ring neck Pheasant. Neither men are wearing a tie, but the same man with the hat has a gold pocket watch and chain tucked into his left vest pocket. The woman seated next to the hatted man is wearing a white silk dress, and from the cut, I would say Paris. Oh, and Akoya Pearl earrings from Japan. The other woman, a pale pink summer dress with small details of yellow crocuses, no jewelry. I did not see her feet when we came in, but from the angle of her legs, she is wearing heels." Fiona leaned away from the table to see if she could catch a glimpse of the ladies legs. Just as Sherlock had surmised, she was wearing heels.

Fiona was amazed at just how accurate he had been, but couldn't help herself, she continued to probe, "And lastly Mr. Holmes, you have the good taste to invite me to dinner." She said it as if the descriptions had not just taken place, and there was absolutely no reason to confirm to the one who spoke without a moment's hesitation anyway.

Sherlock opened his eyes, "Is that what I did when I came into the room?"

She overlooked the lack of tact displayed, for it was not one of his attributes. Instead, she leaned forward and whispered, "You could have hidden in your room I suppose."

"Does Dr. Collinsworth often discuss his patients with you?" Sherlock was not sure if he had said it to test her or put her off.

He was mildly surprised by her answer. "Of course he does. We consult over each and every patient here, you're not that special." She added lightly. "To only talk about you would be unprofessional."

Sherlock was not sure if he was relieved or a little hurt that she might be only interested in him as a patient. Though Dr. Collinsworth had told Holmes about her abilities and his faith in her intelligence, he was a victim of the times. He was having difficulty in coming to terms with the facts that this was a woman who was entrusted with these intimate details. Holmes could see she was not like any woman he had met before. Yes, she was beautiful, and that may be the reason he was so quick to dismiss her, but there was much more to her than what met the eye. He grudgingly had to admit that though she used her femininity as a cover, a mask from which to safely observe from, she was astutely analytical in processing information. That was something he could appreciate, in many ways, she could be his equal in analytic, a thought that had never before occurred to Sherlock.

"Sherlock..." his eyes suddenly shifted. "For a moment there you looked a million kilometers away. What were you thinking about just now?"

Holmes was slightly embarrassed that he had taken a momentary flight of fancy. To cover himself he took up his wine glass in a toast, "Here's mud in your eye." then took a sip.

This phrase had truly caught her off guard, and she started to giggle in delight. "Where in the world did you ever hear an expression like that?"

Without thinking about it, he said, "From a ruffian who drank a cup of poison rather than being arrested for murder and finding justice on the gallows."

"Really, do you often associate with murderers Mr. Holmes? She had said this teasingly, but he suddenly wondered why he had said it too. He could tell she was asking as a clinician, again her demeanor hiding her actions. Before Sherlock could respond, he spotted Anthony Colton coming through the doors, stopping as he entered, then panning the room, but for what Holmes questioned. Then from across the dining hall, their eyes met, locking onto each other. Colton's eyebrows narrowed, his eyes cold and lifeless like a cadaver. Holmes braced himself as Anthony began to weave through the slalom course of tables in the dining room towards his corner of the dining room. Holmes' slight body tension and change of expression was not missed by Fiona.

Anthony Colton stopped a few feet shy of Miss Wilcox, her back was to him. "Good evening Mr. Holmes, Miss Wilcox." His voice light and airy as if greeting old friends.

Fiona turned in her chair to see who had greeted them. "Why Anthony, good evening, would you care to join us?"

Colton smiled ingratiatingly at Miss Wilcox, "I would be delighted, thank you." He began to sit in the chair next to Fiona while glancing at Sherlock, looking for some sort of reaction.

Fiona quickly picked up on the tension between the two men. She conjured up a false gaiety asking, "Do the two of you know each other?"

Holmes waited to see how Colton would answer the question. Anthony studied Sherlock briefly, then turned his head to Miss Wilcox. He leaned closer in an intimate way, dripping with charm, "Oh, we met the other day, and then again from across a chess board." His expression of sociability melted into contained fury, and just as quickly the facade returned. He turned his attention to Sherlock while still speaking to Fiona, "He is quite an accomplished chess player." The fake smile still held on his countenance.

She prompted him, "Is he?" she wanted to see where this was going, her full attention to each word spoken.

"Yes, I took a savage beating by his hands, but, I will get even."

Holmes could not miss the double meaning to Anthony Colton's words. "We shall see about that." Letting Anthony know he understood completely. Fiona too realized from their body language that there was something amiss.

****

Dr. Collinsworth came into the hall and immediately spotted the trio together. In his alarm, he quickly crossed the room. Sherlock noted the Doctor's surprising agility maneuvering around the dinner guests. This time greetings were cut short in an attempt to put himself between two potential combatants. Even before arriving at the table he called out,"Do you mind one more at your table?"

Neither Holmes nor Colton replied, but it was Fiona who welcomed him,"For you, always." Her genuine smile was inviting.

As he drew near, he leaned down to give her a kiss on the cheek. They shared a very brief exchange of eye contact that stated something was going on here, understood from years of working together. "Mr. Holmes, Mr. Colton." He said as he slid into the seat between the two men. "So what is the dinner conversation tonight?" The doctor's countenance feigned lightness as if they dined together nightly.

Fiona's effervescence bubbled over, "Chess. We are talking about Chess. Isn't that right gentlemen?" A question within a question.

Collinsworth declared, "Quite the challenging game I must say. I too long have suffered at the hands of Anthony here." Collinsworth looked at each man, "I understand the two of you had an exciting match." Anthony could not hold back a glare, he looked like he could boil over at any moment.

Sherlock coolly declared, "I took advantage of an early error on Colton's part."

Dr. Collinsworth wanted to get away from this line of conversation before there was a scene. "Does anyone know what they are serving for dinner tonight?"

Since no one had bothered to ask, they just looked awkwardly at each other for a few seconds before Holmes broke the impasse, "I'm sorry Doctor, other than the steward bringing out the wine, which I must say, my compliments on the selection, we have no idea. I am sure whatever it is, it will be as splendid as any meal we have had the pleasure of enjoying before."

An uncomfortable silence ensued, while the other tables chattered not knowing the tension at this one. Fortunately, the parade of carts started to roll, and the meal was placed before them, roasted chicken, boiled baby potatoes, and a Caesar salad. A nice complement to a warm summer day.

Few words were spoken as they ate their meal. Mostly knowing glances were passed back and forth. Anthony Colton consumed his food like he was in a prison camp and at any moment someone might try to take what he has. He finished well before the others had reached the mid-point of their meal. Laying down his fork, he rose said good night and walked away, as three pairs of eyes watched him leave.

Fiona sighed, "Well that was awkward." She looked to them for their response.

"I suppose he didn't like losing to me," Holmes said

"I'm not blind Mr. Holmes, I think there is much more to it than that. What are you not telling me?" A fire kindled in her eyes.

Holmes made a quick glance at Collinsworth then slowly shook his head, "I wish I knew, I really do."

She was not convinced with his act. The fire grew in her as she bored in on Collinsworth, "Doctor, what light can you shed on this?" A question that left no room for anything but the truth.

He squirmed in his seat like he had been sitting on a sack of rocks. "I don't know or have any concrete information to confirm it, but I think Anthony knows Mr. Holmes from some time in the past before his arrival here. And that, my dear, concerns me, concerns me greatly. That being said, I want you to be careful around Anthony. Mr. Holmes thinks, and I tend to agree, that by association for whatever reason, you are possibly at risk."

She glared at the two of them, "Fine, but don't either one of you keep me in the dark. Is that understood?"

Chapter 11

The beautiful weather of three days ago was now replaced by more typical English temperatures and clouds. What was once brilliant blue before was now covered in dull gray hues as the windswept clouds streamed across the sky. The few residents outside were bundled in overcoats and scarves whereas before the attire was light and airy.

Sherlock was sitting on the veranda waiting for his tea order and thinking about his previous daily session with Dr. Collinsworth. He felt frustrated that he still could not remember what was said during hypnosis. According to the doctor, he freely could relate specific details about his life when prompted, but after coming out of the hypnosis, though instructed, he was unable to recall even the slightest memory. Collinsworth would feedback the words spoken, his life history in intimate detail, but to Holmes, he was describing a life that belonged to someone else. There was some missing piece of the puzzle, some clue that was escaping him.

Sherlock physically sank into his seat, his chin pressed against his chest, eyes locked onto the hands that were clasped in his lap. He emptied his mind of external clutter. Like a photograph that lays in a tray of developing chemicals, a picture that is ghostly, unformed, out of focus and just out of reach taunted him. His thoughts came back to Anthony Colton. Colton knew something about him. Sherlock was certain Colton was somehow linked to him from his past. He considered the option of confronting him but knew instinctively that was the wrong avenue to take. Anthony would not freely give up any secrets that gave him an advantage. Instead, Holmes would step back and observe. He knew it was there, somewhere in his mind, locked away, The key, a trigger, a moment in time that would free him from this pitch black cave he found himself in.

Holmes' thoughts were interrupted by a pair of legs coming up the steps. He lifted his head from his chest to see Dr. Collinsworth approaching him. "There you are, Holmes. I thought I should check in on you. You seemed discouraged when you left my office this morning, but I have good news for you." He reached the last step and sat at Sherlock's table. At that same moment, the tea arrived. The staff must have seen the Doctors approach because there was an extra cup on the tray. Holmes poured tea for Dr. Collinsworth and himself.

"Tell me, doctor, what has you smiling like a Cheshire Cat?"

"Reggie has located a Dr. Watson, quite by accident. In his inquiries, he came across a landlady who knew him very well. She lets a property to him at 221B Baker Street in London. Does that ring a bell?" Holmes just shook his head. "No matter, this Dr. Watson is en route to our facility as we speak. He told Reggie that indeed he knows you quite well, and was understandably shocked to find out that you were here. Holmes, he thought you were deceased. I don't have all the details as to why he thought that, but for now, let us rejoice in this happy turn of events. This could very well be the breakthrough we need to bring back your memory." Sherlock was strangely quiet. "I thought you would be pleased to hear this."

"I suppose I am, it's good to confirm that Dr. Watson is not a figment of my imagination, and the address you gave, perhaps it should mean something to me but it doesn't. Why doctor, why am I still unable to make any progress?"

"I understand Holmes. This is a process and will take time. When it comes, things can change rapidly. His presence or his information could very well burst the dam, and you will be 'right as rain.'"

"I wish I could share your enthusiasm," Sherlock said stoically.

Dr. Collinsworth reached out his hand and placed it on Sherlock's shoulder, "Trust me, Holmes, I've seen this scenario many times before, you'll see."

"Do you know when Watson will arrive?" Sherlock was trying to rally.

"The train is due at the station by three O'clock. Reggie will be there to greet him, then he'll bring him straight away by hansom. By four O'clock Holmes, we might start to find some answers. Please be encouraged."

Sherlock let his emotions show by sighing and letting the tension drain from his body. "Thank you, Doctor, I know you are doing your best, and I truly appreciate that very much."

The Doctor stood up, "I will leave you to collect your thoughts. When Dr. Watson arrives, I will have him come into my office and Reggie will inform you when we are ready to have you come." Collinsworth winked at Sherlock with a half smile, "Until then Holmes."

The doctor exited the porch through the double doors leading into the foyer, while Sherlock finished off the last swallow of tea. He too rose and sought refuge in the peaceful gardens.

Chapter 12

4:27 pm Holmes looked at his pocket watch for the third time. He paced the room starting from the fireplace mantle to the door leading out to the hall, seventeen times there and back, fourteen steps without variation. Sherlock was not going to admit to himself to being nervous though his action stated the contrary.

A knock at the door broke the spell, "Come in please." He spoke placidly.

Reggie Clifton poked his head in through the open door, "Dr. Collinsworth and Dr. Watson are ready for you now Mr. Holmes." He smiled warmly at Sherlock, "A bit of marvelous luck finding him. I hope it all goes well for you sir." Reggie retreated back through the door.

Sherlock took a quick glance in the armoire mirror, tugged on his jacket and closed the door behind him. As he walked down the hall, he wondered what lay ahead. Would he get his life back as the doctor postulated? This time the passage through the hallways seemed much longer. Coming to Dr. Collinsworth's door,

Holmes gripped the knob and breathed deeply before turning it. Once inside Sherlock was greeted with a pair of beaming faces

"My God Holmes." Watson's voice rose to a crescendo, "I didn't believe it could possibly be true when Reggie Clifton contacted me, but here you are." Watson crossed the room quickly in broad strides. He took hold of Sherlock's hand and pumped it for all it was worth; Holmes stood still with a confused expression. It suddenly occurred to Watson that Sherlock did not recognize him. "My dear friend, what has become of you, do you not know me?" Watson started to laugh nervously, "Oh Holmes, this is no time for games." Watson could see Sherlock was struggling to remember. He could see it in his eyes. Watson turned to Dr. Collinsworth, "You said he had a memory loss, but this! I'm his closest friend; we shared an apartment together for God's sake."

Finally, Sherlock spoke, "Watson my good man, let us sit down and explore this further. It does no good if you start running around the room and rant." Watson was taken aback by Holmes saying this. It sounded so like what Holmes would have stated in any other circumstance.

Sherlock looked to the doctor, "Doctor, I think Watson here could use a stiff drink, wouldn't you say?" Holmes was calm, considering what was taking place.

"You are quite right Mr. Holmes; perhaps it would do us all good to join him. Please make yourself comfortable, and I will be with you momentarily."

Sherlock took the seat that he customarily sat in during his sessions with Dr. Collinsworth and Collinsworth noted how much Sherlock was a creature of habit in occupying that very same chair. Watson unconsciously moved to the leather sofa and sat on the far right side nearest Holmes needing to be near his friend. Even his posture as he sat on the very edge of the cushion said volumes to Dr. Collinsworth. The doctor remained by the cabinet giving them space, taking his time pouring the drinks.

Watson leaned closer, his elbow pressed against the armrest for support. His voice just above a whisper, "Holmes look at me, surely you must know me." His eyes were pleading for a positive response.

"Watson, I sincerely wish that this was the case, you have no idea how maddening it is not to know one's self, much less having a close friend come face to face and yet draw a blank. Dr. Collinsworth tells me details of my life that I relate to him during hypnosis that means nothing to me. I feel as if I am in a deep well and someone has nailed a lid on top."

Watson did his best to reassure Sherlock, "Holmes I will always be here for you regardless of how long it may take. I promise you; you are not alone in this any longer."

Dr. Collinsworth had waited for this moment to pass before bringing the drinks to Holmes and Watson. He handed the shot glasses out, lifted his, "Gentlemen" As he looked at each man, "I would like to propose a toast." The men looked at him expectantly, "To the days yet to come, and new light shed. May Sherlock Holmes no longer be sick in the head."

There was a moment of stunned silence before all three of them burst out laughing. Collinsworth knew how important it was to break the tension in the room.

Watson settled back into the sofa. He sipped from his glass enjoying the warmth of the liquor sliding down his throat. Then he casually stated, "Holmes, I can hardly wait to let people know that you are alive and well, your brother Mycroft... " Sherlock cut him off with an emphatic 'no' Watson was stunned, "I, I don't understand, there are people who should know you are alive."

Sherlock replied forcefully, "Be it as it may, until I am myself, I prefer to keep this quiet, and under no circumstances are you to reveal my presence here to anyone. Can you do that Watson?"

"Yes Holmes, I will do exactly as you request. As fortune would have it, I hurried here as soon as I found out and did not disclose to my wife where I was off to. I will concoct a story that she shall accept. After all, it wouldn't be the first time that I had to do so." Sherlock did not understand the reference. Watson chuckled, "It was you, Holmes, who has dragged me away on your adventures on more than one occasion, much to the chagrin of my wife."

Dr. Collinsworth asked, "Dr. Watson, would you briefly tell us about Holmes, we can get into details at a later time. But for now, a summary would do just fine."

"As I told you earlier before Holmes came in, we have known each other for many years and spent countless hours going over cases in his apartment. You see, Sherlock Holmes is the greatest forensics detective in all of England, for that matter, the world as far as I can tell."

"Fascinating." The Doctor said as he sat straighter in his seat. "That would explain my impressions of Holmes' character, his instincts, and intuition. Many of the details during our sessions now make sense. Dr. Watson, do you know of the circumstances of Holmes' disappearance?"

"As a matter of fact, I do. We were in pursuit of a very dangerous criminal while on the Continent. It was there that Holmes had confronted him, while I had been sent back down by Holmes' command. When I returned, there was plenty of evidence of a great struggle. It was my assumption that both of them had lost footing and plunged over the Reichenbach Falls. That Dr. Collinsworth was over a year ago."

Sherlock sat listening to what was being said, totally at a loss of what to think. None of it triggered any new memory. It did though explain why he thought as he did. Even that little bit encouraged him greatly. Though never stated nor given much credence in his mind, he no longer thought that he might be crazy.

"Okay, Gentlemen." The Doctor started, "This gives me some excellent ideas about which direction to take. I have a feeling we are not that far from unlocking the truth, and at some point, returning his memory. I suggest we leave it there for today and meet again tomorrow, shall we say ten O'clock? Dr. Watson, of course, you will stay with us. I will have Reggie arrange for your accommodations.

Chapter 13

Sherlock Holmes was restlessly wandering his room, and dinner was not for another hour. "I need to move so I can think clearly," he thought, so he left his room and started down the hall at a very casual pace taking his time to look at the artwork on the walls. Whoever was responsible for the selections, was enamored with French Impressionism. The oil he viewed in front of him was a Claude Monet, Soleil Levant. The blend of blue and gray melding into each other was soft and serene. Holmes realized just how well funded this institution must be. He could tell this was no copy but the original painting. There were other works by artists he was not familiar with, perhaps some who would one day be well known.

Holmes was now on the second floor making his way to the far end. At this level, there was an alcove that was directly above the foyer. There were doors to a balcony that gave the same view to the gardens as Dr. Collinsworth's office. The drapes covered most of the windows and door allowing only filtered light through. The primary source of light was from a pleasant fire burning, giving a soft amber hue reflected off the walls. Above the mantle was another Monet original, "Woman with Parasol." The blends of muted colors layered over each other were pleasing to Holmes. He wondered if the institution owned these paintings or were on loan. Sherlock did not think that he was one who took particular interest in art but knew it none the less. He supposed it might have to do with what Dr. Watson had said earlier.

Since Sherlock had the room to himself, he sat in the overstuffed chair nearest the fire. He placed his feet on the matching ottoman and took out his pipe. The ritual of filling the bowl and tamping in the tobacco with his thumb felt somehow reassuring. Striking the match on the silver box, it gave off a slight sulfur aroma wafting up to his nostrils. Even that was something that tickled the edges of his memory. Drawing in the flame, igniting the tobacco, the bowl of the pipe glowed red for a moment. He inhaled the acrid but sweet smoke into his lungs, holding it momentarily then releasing it ever so slowly through his nose.

Sherlock stared at the fire lost in thought, seduced by the familiarity of pipe, his revery was broken by a voice just outside the room. There stood Dr. Watson wearing a brown vested gabardine suit in a wide plaid pattern. His right hand buried in his pocket as if he were digging for some item. "My God Holmes." Watson's voice choked with emotion, "Seeing you sitting there with a pipe in hand, and legs stretched out by the fire, is a scene

I've witnessed a thousand times before in your apartment on Baker Street. You even have the same expression you always get when you are deep in thought. It's as if time has overlapped with the past and this last year had never happened."

Calmly Sherlock suggested, "Come sit Watson, you look unstable."

"It's just, that I can't believe I'm here with you Holmes," Watson said as he came into the room. He sat in the seat next to Sherlock never taking his eyes off him, perhaps afraid this was only a dream, and if he looked away the image would melt into nothingness.

Sherlock's eyes bored into him reminiscent of the many times his professors had just before they would ask a difficult question. "Understand Watson; I don't remember you. What you said or might say yet to come, perhaps will mean something, but right now, I need you to remain calm." Sherlock gave a reassuring smile, "Consider it an adventure." Sherlock sank into the cushions and gave renewed attention to his pipe looking completely relaxed.

It was necessary for Watson to take a few deep breaths, releasing them slowly to feel on equal with Holmes finally, as his features softened dramatically. He watched Sherlock quietly for a minute or two, no words passed between them. Holmes smoked as if he hadn't a care in the world; this was just one more truism of Sherlock's' character. Watson thought there was so much to say, and so many questions left unanswered.

He could not contain himself any longer, "Holmes, the last time I saw you we were in hot pursuit of Professor Moriarty…" Watson had not said the name before in the doctor's office. Sherlock literally jolted in his seat, his pipe suddenly abandoned. Watson could tell instantly that the name meant something to Sherlock.

Holmes said the name with both a question and an exclamation, "Professor Moriarty."

Watson leaned forward hopefully, "Do you recall the name, Holmes?"

"Tell me what you know about him, Watson," Sherlock's interest peaked.

Watson could see the light aglow in Sherlock's' eyes. The same light of old when he was gathering clues where others saw nothing. "Professor Moriarty was a master criminal, responsible for much of the nefarious activity throughout the streets of London. His criminal organization had roots in murder, theft, extortion, drugs, and many other sordid crimes committed in the underbelly of a great society. We had been on his trail halfway across Europe in an attempt to undermine his toppling of a foreign government. We pursued him to Reichenbach Falls in the

Bernese Oberland region of Switzerland. We were literally on a goat trail when a letter came by a messenger for me. You sent me back to the village of Meiringen, Holmes. That was the last time I saw you. When I returned and went further up the trail, there was a spot where a great scuffle had taken place and, judging by the imprints; apparently, you and Moriarty had fallen over the edge locked in mortal combat. And yet, here you are!" his voice had risen several octaves in the telling. Then he sat back in his chair, drained by his emotions.

"Easy Watson, just the details, tell me, what did Moriarty look like?"

Watson grew confused, "Well Holmes, I never actually had seen him before."

Sherlock was surprised, "You mean to tell me, while we covered Europe, never once did we get close enough for me to identify the criminal to you?"

"No Holmes, he always was just one step ahead of us, escaping our traps at the last second. You though seemed to take it in stride and were always thinking ahead to the next move on the chessboard. Had it been me, I would have been extremely put out." Though the intensity still glowed in Sherlock's eyes, he casually crossed his legs on the ottoman and puffed away like the Orient Express, not saying another word.

The minutes past quietly, only the crackle of the fire broke the stillness. Watson studied Holmes from a side glance, in so many ways he was still the same Sherlock Holmes he had always known, a bit gaunt, but then hadn't he been that way before? What happened up there on that mountain? How could he have had survived the falls, for that matter, how was it he ended up back in London a year later? Watson was committed to finding these answers now that Sherlock was safely back. He wanted nothing more than to have his close friend back as well.

Out of the blue Holmes said jovially, "I'm famished Watson, what say we storm the dining room and see what trouble we can get into." With that Holmes popped up like a Jack-in-the-box and lead Watson out of the lounge.

Chapter 14

Seated at the table, Watson's back was to the room. Curiously he saw the expression on Sherlock's' face change, a new and unfamiliar look of pleasure. He was about to ask the reason when he realized Sherlock's eyes were following someone. His unspoken question was answered by a feminine voice from behind.

"Good evening Mr. Holmes." Said a voice filled with confidence and sweetness too. Sherlock stood, a courtesy Watson had not seen in him before.

Watson also stood up and was turning as Sherlock spoke to her, "Miss Wilcox, May I introduce to you Dr. Watson, whom I'm told is a close personal friend."

Fiona extended her hand gracefully to Watson. "A pleasure Dr. Watson." Her smile was captivating, and Watson returned it with his own. "You're joining us this evening I hope?"

"I would not want to interfere with your reunion," She spoke a bit coyly.

Watson laughed merrily knowing instantly he probably couldn't keep her from Holmes even if he wanted to. "Nonsense Miss Wilcox."

"Fiona," she said.

"Fiona, you grace our table by your presence. Please let me seat you." Watson pulled out the chair just to the right of Sherlock that was between the two men. She came around the table smiling at Holmes and floated into her seat. All the while Sherlock watched her every move without another word. Then he realized he was the only one still standing, so he sheepishly took his seat with a look of confusion. Watson quite enjoyed this new aspect of Sherlock's life. He could not recall a time when there was a woman that held Holmes' interest. Was she a friend, or was there more to this? He would have to watch closely.

There was an awkward moment of silence that hovered before Fiona said, "Dr. Collinsworth has told me all about your arrival and his meeting with you and Mr. Holmes earlier this afternoon. I'm so happy we were able to find you and have you come. I anticipate we'll have good results in the near future. Surely you will be able to assist Holmes in reconstructing his past, and before you know it, you will have your friend back, and as Dr. Collinsworth likes to say 'You'll be right as rain.'" She said that last part with a smile directed at Sherlock that was disarming and genuine.

Their brief conversation was interrupted by a server, a young man of about the age of twenty. He had with him a tray with a fiasco bottle containing a Red Italian wine and three glasses, "Dinner is still about fifteen minutes away, so I thought you might like to start with this. Is there anything else I can do for you?"

Sherlock observed that the server spoke only to Fiona and never took his eyes off of her the entire time. Oddly he became aware of a slight feeling of possessiveness and even a tinge of jealousy coursing through his veins. For that brief moment Sherlock was immobile and at a loss for words. It was left to Watson to dismiss the young server, "Thank you, mighty decent of you to think of us, my good man." The server gave a slight nod and withdrew.

Fiona turned to Watson, "So tell me, Dr. Watson," Fiona's eyes shined brightly, "You must have many fascinating tales of your adventures with Sherlock Holmes." She glanced at Sherlock flirtatiously, "After all, I'm told he is a great detective, and Scotland Yard is lost without him."

Watson was taken aback by her statement, "I never said Scotland Yard was lost without him."

"Oh, but it was implied, however." Watson now understood that Fiona was not just a pretty package, but rather her intuitiveness and intelligence that had sparked Holmes' interest in her.

Over the next twenty minutes, Watson regaled Fiona with brief descriptions of but a few cases in which he and Sherlock had participated in. How Holmes would assemble the facts and disseminate a conclusion few could arrive at. She would occasionally ask a detail or two but for the most part just listened.

Sherlock Holmes sat back in his chair with the wine glass in hand wordlessly hearing his life revealed to another person. Snapshots of images here and there flashed before his eyes, too out of focus to make much sense. The words Watson spoke felt like they had to be true. Deep down within, Sherlock sensed that it did fit with what he knew to be his core. So in that, he would take solace and be encouraged with what was yet to come.

Chapter 15

Over the next seventy-two hours, meeting in the morning and mid-afternoon, Holmes and Dr. Watson held sessions in Dr. Collinsworth's office. Collinsworth liked having set up a more informal atmosphere, Each meeting was clustered around the fireplace with the furniture moved closer giving a sense of intimacy that men would be comfortable with. The threesome often felt free to smoke, whether pipe or cigar. There were no rules on having a stiff drink even if it was ten o'clock in the morning. Dr. Collinsworth thought if the setting was more like a gentleman's club, Sherlock could feel more at ease.

Each session would entail Dr. Watson recounting some part of Sherlock's past, some were the cases they worked on together or times when they cloistered within the walls of Sherlock's home on Baker Street. He talked about how sometimes Holmes would ask Watson his thoughts on a particular clue like an instructor testing his student. Then he would lead Watson through the correct outcome and why he had missed the mark.

Every once in a while, Dr. Collinsworth would ask a question for clarification or pick up on a detail he thought might help Holmes recall the event. Other times his questions were for his satisfaction of curiosity.

As these events were spoken, Sherlock sat quietly and appeared calm on the exterior. What was going on inside was a different matter. He felt turmoil and anxiety over the fact that none of this was making anything clearer in his mind. Collinsworth watched Holmes struggle with this. He tried to give reassuring words to Sherlock and made the point that cumulatively, the relating information should find its way through the mental blockage.

As Watson continued, Sherlock seemed to draw into himself. Finally, he ushered in a strained voice "Do you have any idea how I feel hearing these stories and yet still drawing a blank?"

"Do you want me to stop Holmes? I could never forgive myself if I caused you pain." Watson was feeling how hard this was for Sherlock and as a true friend, he could not bear being the one to cause his friend to suffer.

Collinsworth was silent, waiting for Sherlock's response. Holmes resigned to his fate mumbled in a whispered voice,"No."

Later Watson got to the final tale in the sequence of events. It was the recalling again of their pursuit of Professor Moriarty. He repeated what he had said days earlier in the lounge with Holmes. While he spoke in detail, Sherlock had been puffing on his pipe furiously like a runaway locomotive, "And so Holmes and Moriarty plunged over the falls together, but somehow Holmes survived while Professor Moriarty met his demise in a watery grave."

Sherlock jumped out of his seat and began pacing the room in a quick step. His eyes blazed with fire, "He's not dead."

Watson was surprised by Sherlock, "What do you mean Holmes, of course, he is."

Sherlock collapsed back into his seat, he bodily drew into himself, "He's not dead. He's not dead" Holmes said over and over again. Watson gave Collinsworth a worried look. What was happening with Sherlock?

Dr. Collinsworth's voice remained calming, "Can you tell us why you believe he is not dead?"

Sherlock stared into the fire, his words barely audible, he continued to repeat that same phrase as if the needle was stuck in the same groove on a record. Collinsworth glanced at Watson, "Dr. Watson, perhaps we could step outside of the room for a moment?" When they rose, Sherlock gave no notice of their leaving.

Watson was stunned, "Doctor, what did I just witness in there? I have never seen him like that before."

Dr. Collinsworth took a moment to ponder, his hand rubbing his chin in reflection. "It is my opinion that this Professor Moriarty is the key to his state of mind. You said Holmes was very responsive when you said the name before. Now when you indicated that Moriarty was dead, Sherlock reacted in the most extreme way possible. It was not the trigger I was hoping for."

Defeated Watson asked, "How do you propose to continue from here?"

"We need to tread softly. I have seen this in a patient before but not in a manner of this intensity. Unfortunately, I pushed too hard, and he was not ready to face his demons yet."

"What became of the patient?" Watson feared to ask.

"He is still residing here with us, and just this year he has started to feed himself with a spoon. It took the better part of five years to get to that point." Watson felt the words as if he were struck with a club. His hand reached out to find the wall. His knees almost buckled. Dr. Collinsworth took hold of Watson's right arm holding him up. "Steady doctor, take deep breaths and exhale slowly."

Watson hadn't cried since he was a child, but tears filled his eyes, "I can't lose him again doctor, not after being reunited. I know he is in there, I saw it. Tell me this is merely a setback."

"I honestly wish I could say this is only a bump in the road, but I'm afraid I can't promise a full recovery. I am always hopeful and expect patients to recover, but sometimes the hurdles are beyond the capacity of the patient."

****

Watson led Sherlock back to his room. Holmes followed obediently but silent, his eyes looked dull and lifeless. His skin felt clammy and cold. Watson put Holmes into a straight back chair placed near the window so he could see out into the outer world. "I will check back on you later to see how you are doing. Rest now." Watson wasn't even sure Holmes could hear him. His look was far away, further than he had ever witnessed before when Holmes was lost in his thoughts in front of his fireplace.

Later that afternoon, Watson came back as promised to find Fiona Wilcox reading to Holmes. He stood there a few moments watching them before greeting Holmes and Miss Wilcox, asking how Sherlock was feeling at this time, but what he received was vexing. Holmes was indifferent to Watson, not even acknowledging his presence. He decided it better to leave, for now, so he closed the door as quietly as possible so as not to disturb them.

Then Dr. Watson returned to Collinsworth's office. He knocked on the door hoping the doctor would be available. Watson was answered with a warm greeting and handshake. "Come in, we have much to talk about. You look like a man who could use a drink."

They sat again by the fireplace, Collinsworth waited for Watson to speak. Watson looked wounded to the soul, his eyes pleading. "I just left Sherlock Holmes' room. Fiona was reading The Times to him. He would ask pointed questions when an article struck his interest. He seemed fine, except when I first entered he not only didn't know me, but he spoke as though we had never met."

"I'm sorry, this must be very difficult for you. I was concerned that Sherlock's response was a substantial setback. We will need to proceed with more caution from here on out. I will ask you something that will require an act of great faith on your part."

Watson interrupted, "You must know, I will do anything you ask. It breaks my heart to see Holmes like this." Watson leaned forward, "I can see it in your eyes Doctor, you were about to tell me something that..." Watson couldn't finish, his emotions getting the best of him.

"Dr. Watson, what I ask of you is that you go home. Sherlock is unable to deal with the reality you presented in the telling of your joint adventures. He has become fixated on a single event.

This Professor Moriarty is the key. You say they both fell into the falls and by some miracle, Sherlock survived. Now we hear from Sherlock that this man also had survived. The trouble is, neither one should have survived the fall, and that is where we find ourselves at this point. I question the validity of this story. Don't get me wrong. I have no doubt that your version is entirely accurate as you know it. It's just that, for some reason, it does not add up. I have a few ideas as to why, but for now, I would rather not say, that is the reason why I ask you to go."

Watson's shoulders slumped, "How do you propose to go from here?"

"I will continue to use hypnosis to circumvent the block he has established if only to find the root cause of his memory loss. Then, depending on that outcome, a decision will need to be made. He has already lost a year to his condition, and if I can't help him improve, then perhaps we will need to do something radical. That being, I'll attempt to wipe the slate clean."

"What exactly does that mean?"

"It means, through hypnosis, I will try to create a bridge in his mind. A way for him to function without the conflict that is debilitating him."

Watson looked surprised, "You can do this?"

"I have used this technique before, but I have to give you fair warning, It's not without risks. Holmes could end up having permanent loss of memory. In other words, he would not be the Sherlock Holmes you know." Watson stared at Dr. Collinsworth in great anguish. "Please be reassured Dr. Watson, I will personally keep you informed of his progress."

"Will I be able to come visit in due time?"

"That will depend on Sherlock's progress of course, but if worse comes to worse, he'll appreciate having a new friend, I'm sure."

Chapter 16

Over the next few months, Dr. Collinsworth was true to his word.

Dear Dr. Watson,

I continue to have mixed news for you. Sherlock Holmes is responding well to treatment. I did, in fact, find it necessary to expunge his memory of your stay here. He still refers to your name at random times and questions himself as to why he can't put the pieces together. I hate to be dishonest by telling him we have yet to locate anyone by that name, but he seems not too terribly troubled by not knowing who you are. His attitude has been most cooperative and accepting of the process in therapy. I think he has come to terms with realizing that this will take time and piece his memory one detail upon another will eventually bear fruit. As an observer, I can already see areas where his memories have come back even though he may not recognize the change yet.

As you might have noticed during your visit here, Sherlock has taken a shine to Fiona Wilcox. She, in turn, has also seemed interested in him. Her help has been invaluable with his treatment, and she has spent many hours during this process to comfort and guide him through the maze of conflicting thoughts.

To my chagrin, however, a byproduct of clearing his memory has had an unintended result. He now seems indifferent towards Miss Wilcox. I don't know for sure, but perhaps, this in truth is simply part of Sherlock Holmes' personality. Could you give me any insight as to whether or not he tends to remain aloof with women in general? Any information you could give me would be helpful. Fiona, though I'm sure disappointed, has remained most professional in her dealings with Sherlock and though we have not talked about her possible feelings for him, she continues with utmost dedication.

Now as to the matter of Professor Moriarty being the key to unlock this mystery that we spoke of during your stay. It was while in a deep state of hypnosis that I asked Sherlock if he could tell me what Professor Moriarty meant to him. His response surprised me. He said and I quote, "We are one, two sides of a coin. The nature of good and evil." As I prodded further, I asked him to try to describe him to me. Holmes seemed to have difficulty, saying the image, "was clouded." I then took him still deeper until he could finally reveal an identity. This is what he told me, "The man was over six feet in height, slender in build, with long narrow features in his face, and an aquiline nose that was distinguishable and unique." Tell me if I'm wrong, but it seems as if he has confused his own features with the professor. Could you enlighten me with your description of the Professor? Otherwise, I'm inclined to speculate that either Sherlock Holmes has acquired a split personality, or Professor Moriarty is Sherlock's alter ego.

Dr. Watson, can you shed any light on this? Can you account for Sherlock's whereabouts during any of these crime sprees that you spoke about? I wait with bated breath.

Your friend,

Dr. Collinsworth

A letter arrived a few days later.

Dear Dr. Collinsworth,

I send you a heartfelt thank you for your exceptional care of my friend. I know he is in good hands. You must understand though my shock at the mere suggestion of Holmes having any possible connection to committing a crime. I know Sherlock Holmes better than anybody else, maybe even better than he knows himself. Trust me when I say he is incapable of doing any act of evil. It simply is against his very nature. I not only would stake my reputation, but I would stake my life on his goodness. Perhaps Professor Moriarty is just as he described him. There has to be a logical answer to these questions. As far as Holmes having an alter ego, I never saw any indication that would give evidence to that state of mind. However, this is your area of expertise and knowing what I have witnessed on the field of battle, I understand how stresses can affect one's well-being. That being said, I'm confident you will discover the truth and restore my friend to complete health. I sorely miss him and hope to see him again in the near future. Please keep me posted, and if there is anything I can do to help you only have to say the word.

Your faithful servant,

Dr. Watson

Similar letters passed between Dr. Watson and Dr. Collinsworth over the next year and a half. Finally, Dr. Watson sent this letter.

Dear Dr. Collinsworth,

How much longer must Holmes live in a state of limbo? As I have said before on many occasions, my wife and I are most willing to provide a home and care for Sherlock. As you expressed in the very beginning, Sherlock Holmes could use a friend, and we miss him terribly.

Your friend,

John Watson

Greetings John,

I understand your frustration and your desire to care for your friend. However, the course of treatment remains a fragile weave through his psyche. Each time I get too near the center of the issue, Holmes reacts in a way that tells me the inner struggle between Holmes and Moriarty is too painful to deal with. It would be helpful if I had any physical evidence or testimony from other sources as to Moriarty's existence. Yet, it's been almost three years since that fateful event on the mountain, and still, no traces have come forth from Scotland Yard. I'm afraid we are at an impasse in his treatment, and I in all good conscience can not allow Sherlock to be put into an environment that might cause a total regression to the state of which he had been when he arrived here.

Trust me when I tell you, Sherlock for all practical purposes is happy here, and we will continue to take the best care possible. My dear friend, I know this is not what you wanted to hear, and it does not preclude your involvement at some later date. I ever retain hope that some conversation or memory will trigger a cascade in his mind and you will get Sherlock Holmes back as you have known him.

Your friend,

Reginald

Dear Reginald,

I must confess though it breaks my heart, I admit defeat. Two years of searching and I have come to a dead end. If Professor Moriarty existed, he had layer upon layer of covering of his deeds and honestly, only Sherlock Holmes has the ability to sift through the clues to a clear conclusion. So, where do we go from here? I can not, nor will not believe that my dear friend will forever be trapped in an asylum.

Your friend,

John

Dear John,

If there is no chance of change in Sherlock's condition, and you feel, as his friend he would be better served living with you and your wife, we must look at one final treatment that would enable Sherlock Holmes to return to you. As you know, we can do a procedure of a lobotomy. Thus ending any risk of relapse. Please advise.

Your friend,

Reginald

Dear Reginald,

In a word, NEVER! I know Sherlock would rather die than lose any aspect of his mind. I continue to put my unending trust in Sherlock Holmes to fight through this no matter how long it takes. If I have to be a friend from afar, so be it. Tell me you will never again suggest this solution.

I know how much you care for your patients, and want the best for them. If he truly is happy there, then that will have to be the way it is.

Your friend,

John

Chapter 17

Sherlock was awakened by the sounds of rapid footfalls coming up the hallway. There was urgency in their wake. A couple of sharp raps on his door confirmed his sense that he was needed. Even before he had the chance to pull the bed covers off, Reggie Clifton came into his room. "I'm sorry to burst in like this Mr. Holmes, but Dr. Collinsworth asked me to personally retrieve you with the greatest speed. I'm to take you to his office the moment you are dressed."

Sherlock quickly moved to his dressing table without lighting the room, dawn was still hours away. He put on only the basics forgoing any formality since time was of the essence. Clifton waited by the door until Holmes was ready. Then they passed through the hallway corridors silently allowing the remaining residents to be undisturbed.

Holmes and Clifton entered Dr. Collinsworth's office without knocking, finding him at his desk with a half-filled tumbler of bourbon in his hand. Sherlock noticed that the doctor had spilled some on his desk while pouring, and the doctor's hand was quite evidently still shaking. Reggie closed the door and stood just behind Sherlock waiting quietly for the doctor to speak. Dr. Collinsworth was taking deep breathes staring off into space, making no move to acknowledge their presence.

Sherlock waited a few moments assessing the situation before speaking, "Dr. Collinsworth, I can safely assume this is not a social visit. If you will unburden yourself from what is troubling you. Then perhaps the load may be a bit lighter. After all that you have done for me, it would be a small payment in return."

Dr. Collinsworth lifted his head facing Holmes, his eyes glistened with tears feebly held back. The Doctor's hair was tousled and uncombed, giving him the appearance of someone who had not slept for some time. In an unsteady voice, the Doctor said, "Come sit with me, Holmes."

Sherlock sat across the desk from him while Clifton remained like a sentry at the door, back straight as a board from years of military discipline. Collinsworth glanced at his drink before saying, "Can I offer you a drink?"

"No, it's rather early in the morning for that, or too late at night in either case," Holmes presented a calm demeanor.

"Not if you haven't been to bed." Collinsworth lifted his glass to his lips and poured the remaining contents down his throat. Sherlock knew that had to have burned going down, but the doctor showed no sign. "Holmes, I have struggled with what I'm about to ask of you, for the last twenty-four hours. In no way do I want to put your mental health at risk? But frankly, I'm at wit's end. Something has happened that is beyond our ability to handle..."

Holmes interrupted, "Please don't worry about me. I understand your concerns, but you would not have brought me here if it wasn't a matter of life or death. So give me the details as you know them."

Sherlock's calmness reassured the Doctor. He also recognized how quickly and easily Holmes had assessed the gravity of the moment. "Fiona Wilcox did not take her scheduled time at the front desk the day before yesterday. No one thought much of it, to begin with. She does so many other duties here, and it is not uncommon for one of the other nurses to fill in on short notice. They thought someone had mixed up a request for a replacement and put another nurse on without further inquiry. However, as the day progressed without any sign of her, we became concerned. Reggie inquired with the other staff members as to her whereabouts or if she had told anyone that she was going to be gone from the building for any reason. When it became apparent that no one had an answer, he began a search for her starting with checking in at her apartment. His knocking on her door received no response, and the door was locked as is our policy here for staff. He then covered the building and grounds thoroughly and reported to me his lack of success in finding her. It was at that point that I decided to use the master key to enter her suite. We knocked again before entering, giving her an opportunity to answer after all she simply could have been in sick in bed and not well enough to send word. When there was no answer, we came calling her name out. Holmes, what we found sent an ice cold shiver down my spine. Now, rather than tell you, please come to her apartment and see for yourself."

The three men quietly made their way through the halls and went down a back stairwell that Sherlock had not previously wandered through because it was the staff wing to the building. They arrived at her door with a small brass nameplate identifying her residence. Dr. Collinsworth took out the key and fumbled with it trying to put the key into the slot. His hands had begun to shake again and managed to drop the key on the floor. Reggie swiftly stooped down and picked up the key saying, "Let me open the door, Doctor." Dr. Collinsworth stepped back to make room for Reggie. Holmes observed the pain and anguish written across the good Doctor's face.

Reggie stepped through the door and turned on the light sitting on a side table just to the right of the door. Dr. Collinsworth waited for Holmes to enter first, then followed in his path closing the door behind him. Sherlock saw before him a modest sized apartment, neatly kept with tasteful feminine touches. There were hand stitched brocade pillows lining the sofa and doilies covered the armrest. On the walls hung many watercolors of landscapes, some renditions of the gardens that Holmes found as his place of solace. These were from the hand of Fiona Wilcox; a talent she had kept to herself. From where Holmes stood, there was no sign of a struggle in this part of the apartment. "This way Mr. Holmes," Reggie said as he led him across the parlor into the next room which was Fiona's bedroom. There, boldly written across the flowered patterned wallpaper, a limerick was scrawled with red lipstick.

The bird has flown her homes

To lit upon the combs

But once you are there

You shall descend the stair

Only then to follow my tomes

The moment Sherlock Holmes saw the Limerick, the black veil across his mind fell away. In an instant, Holmes was back. "It's Anthony Colton," Sherlock stated with certainty.

The shock and realization struck Dr. Collinsworth as a hammer blow. The words sprang from his mouth, "Reggie if you have to tear this place apart, find him." Reggie Clifton raced out the door on a dead run before the last words were spoken.

Dr. Collinsworth looked as if he were about to collapse. "Doctor, sit down here," Holmes pointed to the nearest chair that was by Fiona's dressing table. "We need to talk."

Holmes took hold of the doctor to guide him until he was safely seated. Dr. Collinsworth leaned forward and laid his head on the table. Then covered his face with his arms. His voice sounded as if coming from a deep well, words strained and trembling, "What have I done Sherlock? I should have known that it was only a matter of time." The Doctor paused, but Holmes completely understood what he meant. Small gasps came from Collinsworth trying to fight back the tears. "I've killed her Sherlock. Surely as if I had put a gun to her head, I killed her." He finally broke down and wept bitterly.

"Dr. Collinsworth, all is not yet lost. He wrote this limerick intended for me."

The Doctor lifted his head, eyes red and face tear-stained, "I don't understand."

"I was his cause for incarceration, and this was his way of taunting Scotland Yard before I came on the case."

Dr. Collinsworth suddenly realized Sherlock Holmes was talking about his past. "Your memory Holmes." He spoke with a partial question in it.

"It was the limerick that triggered my memory. I can recall everything, my entire history, who I am, what I am, and what I do." The Doctor rose slowly and took the few steps to Sherlock. Full of emotion, he threw his arms around Holmes and gave him a bear hug. But Sherlock's arms hung at his side, not one for this kind of emotional display. "Doctor, we need to leave for London on the next train. Anthony Colton is not here hiding Miss Wilcox, and I'm afraid you sent Clifton on a wild goose chase. Now, what we need to do, is pack our bags for an indeterminate time away. Does Reggie Clifton have a revolver locked away?"

Yes...yes he keeps one for security reasons. But why Holmes, why would Anthony Colton take Fiona?"

"Not now, Doctor. I will explain everything when the three of us are together on the train." Holmes turned and left the room to pack and give Dr. Collinsworth a moment to collect himself.

Chapter 18

Before daylight struck ground, Holmes, Clifton, and Dr. Collinsworth were packed. A carriage was summoned, and the staff was alerted to cover for their absence. Upon the coach's arrival, the men boarded and settled in as best they could. The ride to the station was harrowing because the two-horse carriage proceeded at best speed. The driver made his whip sing over the horses hind quarters urging them onward, while the men inside held on to whatever would keep them seated and not flung from the cab.

Poor Dr. Collinsworth thought Holmes. The man's eyes protruded out of sheer terror. Sherlock could easily assume he had led a sedate life. Reggie Clifton, on the other hand, found purchase with handholds that firmly kept him in place. His face stoic with a look of determination, and his back as erect as always.

The ride ended not soon enough for Dr. Collinsworth. The coach arrived in a cloud of dust that raced past them as they came to a sudden stop. They departed in a rush, barely having time to grab their grips and run down the platform before the morning train started to move. Reggie was carrying both his bag and the Doctors, he threw them onto the deck then stepped up on the landing. Reaching out he took hold of Dr. Collinsworth's arm and assisted him onto the accelerating train. Holmes jogged along the platform and in a fluid motion swung up effortlessly to where the two men stood. Sherlock turned to Clifton, "I think we could do with a spot of tea, while I get the Doctor settled in our berth." Reggie left them with a nod and an appreciative smile.

Holmes extended his arm, "Dr. Collinsworth, take my arm and come with me."

Once in their berth, the Doctor collapsed, panting and rivulets of sweat coursed down the creases of his face. He pulled out a white kerchief and wiped his brow while Holmes waited patiently. Breathlessly the Doctor said, "I'm too old for this and fear I could inhibit your progress."

Sherlock waited to respond to Dr. Collinsworth until they both were seated behind closed doors. "Don't underestimate what valuable details you might disclose as we pursue Anthony Colton. After all, he has been in your care these many years." Hearing this, Dr. Collinsworth loosened his tie and sat back in his seat while still taking deep breaths.

Reggie Clifton returned shortly with a tray holding a pot of aromatic tea and a pile of warm scones with steam still rising off them. "I thought we might need a bite to eat, who knows when we will have our next opportunity."

Holmes unfolded a built-in table in front of the Doctor. "Like a true military man," he declared as he picked up a scone and ate it without bothering to add any condiments. Pouring from a small pitcher, Sherlock put milk into the bottom of his cup, then added the hot tea. He dropped in a single spoon of sugar and stirred as he began to recount to his fellow travelers, "About six years ago, Dr. Watson and I were called in by Scotland Yard and asked to help with a particular case that completely baffled them. There were several murders, well twelve to be exact, that were all committed by one person. They knew this by the messages always written at the scene of the crime. They were in the form of a limerick. As you well know, a disturbed mind often times operate on a different plane than a healthy person. Anthony Colton was, and is, diabolical. He was driven to taunt the police with obscure clues of his whereabouts and what he had intended to do next." Sherlock paused to butter another scone before continuing. "It was regrettable that they chose to delay contacting me for the better part of a year. Many of those who died, died needlessly. I fail to understand why when faced with information that is beyond your understanding, they continued to stumble in the dark allowing this crime spree to run rampant. It was not until public pressure was put upon them that they finally acted. Had I not been involved in another case that had taken me beyond the shores of England, I would have gone to them straight away to offer my services.

That being said, Dr. Watson and I pursued him by the very clues he had thought could not be interpreted, but in truth, brought us to his lair that was well hidden in the dilapidated area of East London. To view the exterior of his building along the wharf, it looked abandoned. The doors were barred with thick planks nailed across them. The lower windows were also covered, giving the impression that there was no entry point. We inspected the surroundings and found a hidden door, concealed by debris, left to look like it had been randomly tossed there. It, in fact, was a prop to give the casual passer the intended impression.

Watson and I discussed our options and decided to enter as stealthily as possible hoping if he was there we could catch him unawares. If he were not in attendance, we would set a trap upon his return. Once inside, we found it to be unoccupied. Since the windows had been boarded up, we lit candles to inspect our surroundings. I suppose that was why he had everything so covered. Colton could come and go as he pleased and none would be the wiser. So it too worked to our advantage. What we saw inside explained much as to how he could be invisible in plain sight. There were racks of disguises, clothing, wigs, and other miscellaneous props that would alter his appearance.

We placed ourselves in strategical locations and extinguished our lights. Hours passed in total darkness. Then in the wee hours just before dawn, we heard his approach from an unexpected direction. A trap door well concealed in the floor rose. It turned out it was linked to the storm drains that poured into the river. Anthony Colton came up the stairs with a lit candle revealing himself dressed as a woman. I might add, I could not have done a better job myself.

He placed the candle on a counter and moved in our direction. We waited until he had come near us before stepping out from our cover. His surprise recovered quickly as he drew a revolver and fired at me. It was my good fortune his hand had caught in the dress fabric, so when he pulled the trigger, his shot grazed my right side instead of his intended target of my heart.

Watson was pressed to respond in kind. He had his revolver in hand at the ready. Before Colton could fire again, Watson took aim at the hand holding the weapon, fired, and made a clean shot. It disarmed Colton who was about to put a bullet into my chest. He knew if he had made any other attempt to move, it would be his last."

Chapter 19

Dr. Collinsworth could not stifle a prolonged yawn, "What did you mean when you said, not all was lost?"

"Obviously Doctor, the Limerick was meant for me. You only need to read the first line."

"But the rest?" Collinsworth was now ferociously rubbing his eyes.

"The rest is quite simple, and I'm assuming Colton kept it that way because he knew of my memory loss. He figured those remnants of my intuition were still in operation, and with time I would solve the lines of the limerick. Now, as to the second verse, it has two meanings. First, he is referring to the catacombs or storm drains beneath the streets of London. Also, it is giving a point of reference, and that is the entrance to where he wants us to descend. That location is The King's Barber at King's Cross Street."

Reggie asked, "How in the world did you know that?"

"It is the only barber shop in London where the tunnels run under the establishment. I was once there, during an unusually heavy rain, having a shave and haircut. I could hear the water movement beneath my feet, though no one else seemed to notice."

"Amazing," stated Dr. Collinsworth.

Sherlock continued, "The third and fourth verses tell us to go to the bottom of the stairs that are next to the barbershop. And finally, the fifth verse is telling us that what we'll find there, will be the next set of clues." With these words, Collinsworth leaned forward and put his head in his hands conveying his stress. Sherlock looked directly at Collinsworth, "Doctor, Anthony Colton intends this to be a long chase. It is his version of cat and mouse. I expect he will continue this game until he is satisfied, then seek his lust for revenge."

"I don't quite follow your meaning Holmes." The Doctor now looked up at Sherlock.

"It's not about Fiona Wilcox. She is merely a pawn in his own personal chess game with me." Sherlock reached over and picked up his third scone and held it under his nose breathing in the rich buttery aroma. But before sinking his teeth into it, he held it out like a baton suspended in mid-air saying, "We have one very significant advantage over Anthony Colton," he paused for effect., "he does not know of my full recovery, and therefore, we may catch him at his leisure."

It was Reggie who asked the obvious question, but with a smile forming on his face, fully catching the drift, "Meaning?"

"Meaning," Holmes' eyes danced with light, "if Anthony Colton keeps his clues this simple, then we just might find ourselves at the next site before he has the chance to set the stage."

The Doctor looked bewildered, "This is all just too confusing for me Holmes."

"Catch him red-handed, Doctor," Holmes said with a smile.

"But is Fiona alive? Can you tell me that?" The Doctor's voice dropped to a whisper.

Holmes not given to false rhetoric replied, "I'm sorry Dr. Collinsworth, only time will tell. However, he needs us to believe that she is alive and unharmed. So for now, yes I do think Miss Wilcox is relatively safe."

The stresses and physical demands on the Doctor had taken their toll. He felt a certain amount of reassurance, and that was all it took for him to slump into his seat, closed his eyes, then drift off to sleep in a matter of seconds. His breathing came easy, and before long, a soft rhythm of quiet snores emanated from the worn out doctor. Reggie Clifton looked upon the physician as a long time friend saying, "He has not slept since we first realized Fiona's disappearance. I truly think he sees her as his own daughter. Mr. Holmes, I'll do anything, and I mean anything to get her back safely."

Sherlock lowered his voice, "Don't tell the Doctor, but I'm very concerned for her well-being. As odd as it seems, Anthony Colton only kills with purpose. But that doesn't mean he wouldn't do something to try to force our hand. By that I mean, he could injure her if it suited his needs."

"Earlier you were telling us about how it was that you caught Anthony. Would you mind if I heard about the case itself, the twelve murders? That was not information we were given when this whole set up at the institution started. I don't like being kept in the dark. And this is far beyond something that should have been kept secret from us."

"I won't go into great detail, but his twelve victims were all connected to his twisted logic."

"And that was?" Reggie asked.

"The twelve apostles."

"How long did it take to figure that out?"

"Since I was not contacted by Scotland Yard until the twelfth victim, about ten seconds," Holmes stated emphatically.

"What?" Clifton said almost too loud and caused Dr. Collinsworth to stir in his seat.

"Scotland Yard had the twelve names written on a sheet of paper. The answer was right before their eyes. Each name was a name of an apostle, it was the art of simplicity by Colton."

"Then how could you proceed from there?" Reggie questioned.

"Well, once I knew his motive, the next victim had to be Jesus."

"Jesus? Who in the world has the name, Jesus?"

Holmes smiled, "That answer is in your question, "who in the world." Sometimes a clue will come from the most unlikely sources. In this case, it came from reading the Times. An article jumped out at me that a long-anticipated art showing at the National Gallery by a famous Hispanic artist by the name of Jesus Marquez was opening in a few days."

Reggie Clifton interrupted, "Jesus?"

"But it's pronounced Hay-sues," Holmes had used "Jesus" for effect first.

"Oh" Reggie still had a baffled expression. "But how did you know it was Anthony Colton?"

"A person does not become a psychopathic killer overnight. Again it was the limericks that made the connection. Some years earlier a case of mysterious deaths of animals within a few miles of Balmoral Castle in Scotland had the neighboring community up in arms. At first, it was made to look as if they were just mishaps. But as time went on, subtle clues were left behind to the confusion of the local constable. Soon the perpetrator became bolder and started leaving messages in the form of limericks. It was quite by accident that he was caught in the act by a crew of farmhands in the predawn while constructing a limerick on the barn wall. Colton was saved from prosecution by the intervention of the royal family and sent off to France.

While on a case not too far from there, I came across that same constable telling another constable the story in a local pub. Though he kept his voice low, I heard the details of the crimes and the outcome. When he whispered the name too quietly to hear, I lip read it was Anthony Colton. I knew this was information that needed to be remembered because sooner or later he would act out again, and that is why I said it was so unfortunate that Scotland Yard had not contacted me earlier.

It was only a matter of tracking down where Anthony Colton was hiding. Fortunately, not knowing that I knew of his past, lived out in the open not fearing disclosure. Watson and I located him within a day, then we hung in the shadows until we could piece together what he was up to. Several times we followed him to the wharf but only to lose him each time mysteriously. It became a process of elimination where he disappeared into. When I had narrowed it down to the last building, we were running out of time, I suggested to Scotland Yard's Inspector Lestrade to place guards to safely protect Marquez. That left Watson and me to seek out the final clue of his lair, and its entry. The rest I have already told you."

"That is remarkable Mr. Holmes."

Holmes said prophetically, "I was not completely honest with Dr. Collinsworth. I believe Miss Wilcox is in grave danger. Colton will kill her in some gruesome way. This would be part of the vengeance visited upon me."

"Because of her association with you, yes?" Sherlock nodded in response. "Then for all our sake, let's not let that happen Mr. Holmes."

Chapter 20

Reggie Clifton and Sherlock Holmes joined the Doctor in slumber, lulled by the rhythm of the train. Not until the sound of squeaking wheels did the three travelers wake, sleep was still heavy in their eyes. Outside the window, their view clouded with steam from the train engine. Passengers moved like ghosts in a midnight fog through a graveyard. The murmurer of human activity blended together with a symphony of life in a big city. Dr. Collinsworth sat up stiff-backed, rubbing his eyes then working out a crick in his neck. "Are we here?" he asked still disoriented.

Reggie stretched out his legs before him, and his arms elevated over his head expelling a high pitched groan. "Yes Doctor, you seemed to have slept soundly. I hope you are somewhat refreshed."

The Doctor looked around and yawned seeing Sherlock sitting placidly as if he had slept in his own bed and already had his morning tea. "Good morning," Holmes said, "we have a long day ahead of us, so we need to be ready as quickly as possible."

Holmes rose and grabbed his bag leaving the berth with the door open.

They crossed the platform to the entry of the station were Holmes said, "We will need a coach and three lamps."

Reggie dropped the bags at his feet and replied, "If you take care to hail a cab, I think I can scrounge up a few lights." He turned away and disappeared into the heavy foot traffic.

"Holmes, shouldn't we secure our accommodations and drop these off?" Collinsworth asked.

"I'm sorry Doctor, there is no time to waste. We'll hire a cab for the day and leave the luggage with the driver." Sherlock picked up his and Clifton's bag leaving Collinsworth to carry his own.

They passed through the station and exited onto the busy street. "How about that one Mr. Holmes?" Dr. Collinsworth pointed to a rather large carriage with the rider wearing a red velvet coat and black stovepipe hat. Harnessed to the carriage were two sleek bodied horses, coal black and brushed to a lustrous sheen. They pawed the earth in readiness to charge the bastions.

The Doctor saw only the luxury of the cab, but Holmes saw the reliability of the steeds. "Good selection Doctor, they shall do fine."

Collinsworth and Holmes went over to the driver, "We have need of your services for the day." Sherlock said. The driver explained his charge and agreed upon a price. Holmes suggested, "Dr. Collinsworth, I advise you to pay him in advance."

They stowed their gear and began looking around for any sign of Reggie Clifton. Sherlock heard the clanking even before he spotted Clifton rounding the corner. He carried with him three soiled lamps. Reggie jumped aboard with his load, bumping the Doctor's knee with one of the lights leaving an oily smug on Collinsworth pant leg. "Oh, I'm sorry, Doc. How clumsy of me." Clifton dropped heavily onto the bench. Dr. Collinsworth stared at his dirty trousers, speechless.

Holmes said while gazing forward, "You will need to be prepared for something much worse Doctor. Where we are going, it will be nothing like you have ever imagined." He asked Colton, "Where did you get the lamps?"

"I thought the conductors shed would be a good place to start. When I explained our dilemma, he parted with them most willingly and wished us God's speed."

"Yes, I assumed that was where they had come from. You did well." Holmes appreciated Colton's abilities.

The carriage moved into the heavy traffic of horse and man. From above one could see it as an anthill, chaos in motion.

Though the going was slow, they had not far to travel because Holmes had chosen the Kings Cross station to start from. The driver brought them to the specified location and stopped just across the lane.

"Now what?" The Doctor asked trying to sound brave but dreading what they might find.

Holmes pointed, "See to the left of the barber shop? That rusty looking gate leads down to the tunnels below."

The men exited the cab and Sherlock said to the driver, "Wait here for the next half hour just in case. Then take our baggage to Brown's on Dover Street and reserve three rooms for us. After which, wait for our arrival for further instructions.

"With private baths, if you please," Dr. Collinsworth rang in. "I have a rotten feeling I'm going to need it."

Sherlock led the way as they crossed the street. When they stood before the gate, Reggie reached out and tried to turn the handle. It held fast. Reggie said, "It sure doesn't look as if it's been opened in years." He shook it and pushed harder. "There is no way anyone has used this entrance."

Holmes calmly replied, "Gentlemen, remember Anthony Colton knows many of the back allies and surely the tunnel system. This was his way of moving about during that time before his arrest on murder charges."

Though still confused, Reggie took several steps backward, then charged ahead driving his shoulder into the gate. It still held. He twice more threw himself at the obstacle before the hinges broke loose and the gate caved in. Each took hold of a lamp and descended the stairs to an iron door. Reggie rubbed his shoulder saying, "I don't think I will have the same results on that monster." Sherlock stepped in front of Reggie with the slightest hint of a smile. He reached out and lifted the latch with two fingers and pushed the door open with ease.

Both the Doctor and Reggie had a look of surprise. Sherlock had a grim smile on his face, "I saw the drops of machine oil on the threshold. Colton had forced the door open from the inside, then oiled it so we could get in. This is his game and here is where we enter to begin.

Chapter 21

The lamps lit, giving off their flickering amber glow. Holmes led the way down the narrow stone steps, followed by Clifton then Collinsworth. Their shadows danced on the walls with the swing of the lamps as if all the ghosts that resided here were accompanying them into the bowels of the earth. The brick was cold and rough to the touch. Years of dankness clung to the surface repulsing the hand from brushing across it, and this was only the beginning.

Dr. Collinsworth silently counted the steps going down. Though they declined thirty feet, he felt as though he had left the world forever and the light of day would never shine upon his face again. Holmes waited at the bottom for the doctor to join him, for he had lagged behind them from the very start. Having reached the bottom, they found themselves in an open chamber, walls curved in a circle and passages led out in several directions.

Sherlock's voice echoed off the walls, "Train your lamps upon the surface. We will find his next clue there."

Dr. Collinsworth gasped out, "Oh my God," nearly dropping his lamp in terror.

Holmes and Clifton moved over to where the doctor was shining his light. There, a shock of red hair hung on a hook hanging from the ceiling. The light breeze that flowed through the tunnel caused it to turn at its whim. "He didn't…," the Doctor choked out, his words barely above a whisper.

"No Doctor. There are no traces of blood," Holmes assured confidently.

Reggie went to the Doctor's side to steady him while he recovered from the initial shock. Meanwhile, Sherlock focused his lamp nearest the bricks looking for… "Here it is, written within this single block."

Follow the rats with the descending sun

Caution it's not safe to run

And when you get there

You shall find no more hair

Oh, is this not jolly good fun

Sherlock turned to the others, "Colton intends to drag us through the muck and mire for his pleasure. Perhaps, Doctor, you would be more comfortable if you returned to the coach and went with the driver to the hotel."

Dr. Collinsworth took in a deep breath and exhaled slowly, "No, I've come this far, and I need to see it through if it's all the same to you." He gave Holmes a weak smile that matched his pale face.

"We will be heading west." Holmes took a moment to get his bearings. "That will be that tunnel there to the right. Dr. Collinsworth, keep your light facing down our path. Clifton, you move your light along the wall on the left side the same way as I do on the right. We are looking for any sign that will direct us." Without another word, he headed that way.

The tunnel amplified their footfalls. It mixed with the ever-present dripping that managed to seep through the brick lining. Their breathing combined to sound like a bellows stoking a blacksmith's fire. These kept them company as they moved further away from the stairwell. Down the center of the tunnel ran a trough eighteen inches wide and perhaps a foot deep. The seepage collected into it and moved slowly with the grade. The doctor walked alongside the trickle of water taking care not to misstep into it while still keeping his eyes ahead. Holmes was to his right and Clifton to his left, they could walk three abreast through this passage.

Up ahead Dr. Collinsworth saw something in his moving light. "What's that?" he stopped and shone the light steadily upon the object.

The other men stopped to see what had his attention. Sherlock said, "There must be a cement company overhead. From the looks of it, they have occupied the place for many years." What they witnessed was a man-made stalactite made from years of lime and silica seeping through until the minerals had formed a column touching from ceiling to floor.

The Doctor commented,"Strange how you can have beauty in a God forsaken place like this."

Another quarter mile deeper in, they came to a y-junction in the path. There was no sign indicating which direction to go. "Clifton, you and the Doctor, go down the left, and I'll go right. Go no more than five minutes. If you don't find anything, we'll come back here and figure out what to do next."

They parted ways and soon were out of sight of each other. Sherlock was carefully looking at the walls setting a slow pace so as to not miss a marker. Then he heard Reggie Clifton call out his name. The sound moved through the tunnel past him and on into infinity. He quickly retraced his steps and followed the others, seeing their lights bouncing off the walls. When Reggie saw Sherlock's light coming, he said, "Over here Holmes. There is a red arrow painted just inside this tunnel."

Sherlock met up with them and shined his light into the smaller space. It was three feet above the floor where they stood, five feet in diameter, and only four and a half feet high. "Okay, I'll go first, then Clifton, and you Doctor shall bring up the rear." He didn't even wait for the others to agree, he climbed in, and with a bent back moved on.

The trio proceeded the next twenty minutes before a voice called out from the back, "Oh for Christ's sake," Dr. Collinsworth had hit his head for the third time in the last twenty minutes. There was no point in consoling him, so they kept moving forward into the darkness, "My back is killing me," the Doctor now complained. Still, no comfort was given.

Then ten more minutes that seemed like hours passed when the Doctor again said, "What in the hell is that awful smell?" This time the other men felt the same way. They finally came to the end of this tunnel. It opened out into another tunnel much like the one they had started in. This time though, there was a large carcass laying in the trough. Its flesh was being eaten by at least a hundred rats scurrying over its body.

Sherlock shed his light on it, "Compliments of Anthony Colton no doubt." Then he jumped down making a number of rats dodge his landing and run from the light. Clifton climbed out and helped the Doctor by giving him his hand.

The Doctor stretched his back and asked, "Now what?"

There was no immediate sign seen, so again they split up with Collinsworth and Reggie going one way, and Holmes heading in the other. This time it took only a moment to find the arrow. "Gentlemen, our next passage is over here." Sherlock waved them back in his direction.

The tunnel was only three feet in height and width. They would either duck walk or crawl depending on how each would approach it. "You have to be kidding me," the Doctor whined. Sherlock held off reminding the Doctor of his previous offer.

"How about I lead this time Mr. Holmes?" Clifton volunteered.

He put the handle of the light into his mouth and pushed himself onto the ledge. He waddled out of site before Holmes could usher the doctor into the confined space. "I'm sorry Doctor, just do your best. I'll be right behind you." The poor doctor disappeared while on his hands and knees.

For the first fifteen minutes or so, the tunnel was dry. Then as they went on, two smaller tubes the size of a bushel, had a steady stream of water leaking out of them. The three men splashed through getting themselves thoroughly wet. Of course, Dr. Collinsworth got soaked crawling. His pants dragged through the water picking up muck as he went along. Just when all hope seemed lost, they again came out into an opening that allowed them to stand.

This time the red arrow was painted boldly on the wall. A tunnel about the same size that the men had just exited invited them with a black mouth. They stood before it and were met with a stench of human feces. "Is that what I think it is?" Dr. Collinsworth sighed.

Since there was no alternative, they entered with resolve. Being no way to avoid it, they soon had what they did not want to imagine on their persons. By now, even Reggie was swearing under his breath. He said to himself, "If I get my hands on Anthony Colton, he won't make it back to the asylum."

As awful as this was, Sherlock knew there was no other way to get the next clue. Colton was in control, and until they had answers, Holmes would follow the leads wherever they lead. He felt the air movement even before they got to the end of this tunnel. Compared to what they were breathing, the following opening was soon to be a relief. "Take heart Doctor, we've reached the end."

The chamber they dropped into was large. It appeared to be a central collection point with a dozen other tunnels emptying into it. Holmes knew they had finally reached the end of this part of the journey, for there was a light source just ahead. Not daylight, but a candle. Pulling the Doctor free from the small tunnel, they took a moment to stretch out the kinks in their bodies. "Let us see what Colton has left for us," Sherlock said as he moved toward the flickering light.

The men gathered around a silver stand with a candle often used by churches. One that would be lit and left to burn for days in hopes of prayers reaching up into the heavenly hosts. It had been there and burning for more than a day judging by how far it had burned down. Holmes knew they must not be too far from the confluence where the storm drains met to deposit the runoff into the river. The air that swirled around them was causing the candle to wave hypnotically. The flame was the last arrow pointing upward to the curve in the stonework. There, several feet overhead was Colton's limerick.

Now for miles you have creep

It is time for you to sleep

You have found your way

It has been a busy day

But tomorrow will be the keep

"How the hell are we going to get out of here," Dr. Collinsworth exploded. "Sorry, that was uncalled for. I'm just tired and could use a stiff drink."

"Colton is finished with us for today. There will be a door or some other exit for us nearby. I suggest we spread out and find it. And yes Doctor, I think we all could stand a stiff drink or two."

It took only a minute to find the door. It too was oiled and free to open. It was Anthony Colton's way of tipping his hat to them. "I don't know if I should be grateful or raging mad that he makes our leaving through here so easy," Clifton said. "I can't stand that he's the cat and we are the mice he tortures until he eats us." That was a feeling all three could agree upon.

Chapter 22

The trio climbed the stairs breathing in fresh air, the daylight burning their eyes until adjusted. Three-mole men who were worn out, stunk, and wet, came to the surface. The streets of London were crowded, and passersby paid no attention to them. This was an area where ordinary workers plied their trade. Dray carts filled the street with crates of vegetables, fruits, barrels of beer, lumber, and stone, ladders and ropes, these were the wares that kept the city alive.

Dr. Collinsworth looked around. This was not a part of the city he had ever ventured into. "Holmes, I must admit the sight of all this food has made me aware of just how famished I am, and, even though we look like something the cat drug in, do you suppose there is someplace we could slip into? Maybe there is a pub nearby? Surely they wouldn't mind our business. Besides, I really could use that drink about now."

They started to weave through the crowds and wagons making their way along the winding avenue. Down the street, they spotted a sign to a pub. "The Wheel -Her- Inn," was three steps down from the street. You had to stoop to enter or else you would end up with a knot on your forehead, as many drunken patrons had done before. No doubt that this at one time was a basement to what was above. The interior was dark and small. Plank board ceiling and walls blackened by years of smokers and cooking smoke. A long counter covered one wall where the barkeep kept his stock. A single barman behind the counter eyed them as they came in. Eight tables, with four chairs each, filled the space. And though it was after lunch, and before supper, half the tables were filled with patrons. Ordering beer was the common choice of drink, each man nursed a pint.

They sat as far away as the small space allowed hoping not to stand out while looking bedraggled. The barkeep came over shortly after they were seated. "Three whiskeys and chasers if you please," said the Doctor. "and could you please bring us menus?"

The keep looked at them like they were foreigners from another part of the world. "Don't have menus. It's all on the board, and if you don't see it, we don't make it." He turned and started walking away without waiting for a response.

"Would you be so kind as to bring us cigars also," the Doctor added.

"Doctor, I don't smoke," Reggie chimed in.

"Right, well Holmes ol' boy, you'll join in won't you. One should not smoke alone. It's just not proper." Dr. Collinsworth was recovering well from their ordeal. He also had the best view of the board and checked out what they could best fill themselves on. Then he saw just what they should have.

The barkeep returned with their drinks and cigars on a small tray. The doctor picked up a shot glass and threw it back lustily. "I'll have another, please. And if my companions don't object, I think we could stand plates of bangers and mash." He gazed at them for approval. No protests were spoken, so the keep left to fill their orders. "You know, it hasn't been since my college days that I have sat down to bangers and mash. I was so poor back then that I'd finish off mine and hope that those with whom I was sitting, would at some point, get up and leave with unfinished plates. Then I would wait until no one was watching and scrape them back onto mine."

Reggie chuckled and was glad that Dr. Collinsworth felt more himself now, but there was business to be taken care of. "What's next Mr. Holmes," Reggie asked. "Anthony Colton has had his fun, but I'm in no mood to be toyed with in his games any longer. His last limerick, I could figure out the first four lines. So, tell us what the meaning of the final phrase is. What is he referring to when he says "keep"?"

"Colton means the Castle Keep. Tomorrow he plans for us to search for the next clue at the Tower of London."

"Do you think he has already put the clues there? Or should I go there and stake out the site. I meant most of what I mumbled in that stinking sewer," Reggie confessed.

"I understand how you feel. I'd be tempted to leave the room for a good smoke while you had a conversation with Colton. But unfortunately in all likelihood, yes I do think he has already been there. I also believe he has an assistant."

Both men were taken aback by that statement. Collinsworth asked, "Why do you think someone is helping him?"

"It is elementary Doctor. First Anthony Colton had to have someone appropriate a carriage in order to spirit away Miss Wilcox. Without one, it would have been nearly impossible. Second, he had that same person prepare those doors for us to open."

"How in the world could you know that Mr. Holmes?" Reggie asked baffled.

"Quite simple really. At both locations, I saw traces of footprints in the muck, and they are smaller than Anthony Colton's shoe size. I would say the other person is no more than five-two, eight stone and seven. Scotland yard always believed he operated alone, but I was convinced he had someone who had the uncanny ability to blend into the background. Colton never once uttered a word to the contrary after his arrest. It is highly probable Colton has been in contact with this person the entire time he has resided with you."

Dr. Collinsworth wondered aloud, "Why now Holmes? Why did he stay at the institute all these years when it appears he could have escaped at any time?"

"He was waiting."

"He was waiting for what Holmes?" Reggie's frustration was starting to show.

"Waiting to complete his murderous cycle. Let me explain. A few weeks ago I was reading in the Times about a small but controversial play scheduled for performances at The Palace Theater. At the time, it meant nothing to me, just a curiosity. But now that my memory has come back. I see the connection." In Holmes' infuriating way he paused to lite his cigar. Then lifted his head skyward exhaling, making rings of smoke drift to the ceiling. "The play," he began again, "is a modern-day version of the life of Mary, that is Mary mother of Jesus. Of course, the church hierarchy had condemned the play even before its opening and made every effort to see that it never see the light of day. That gentlemen, is where our trail will eventually lead us, since finding another person named Jesus is rather difficult. He has replaced him with me. Colton wants me to try and save Miss

Wilcox. I use the word save both literally and symbolically. In Colton's mind, she has taken on the role of Mother Mary. I believe he intends to kill her and me at the Palace Theater."

Reggie Clifton's frustration turned into agitation, "Then why are we running through hoops and not setting a trap at the Theater to catch him off guard?"

"The answer is because we are being watched, even as we speak," Holmes stated in a much lower voice. "Look to your left Clifton, at the bar, last seat at the far end. That is his assistant. After our meal, I want you to say loud enough for him to overhear, that you intend to search on your own and that you will stake out the Tower of London in hopes of spotting Anthony Colton. He will let you go and follow us to be sure we go to the hotel. I want you to double back and trail him after we get to the hotel. Perhaps we may obtain some useful information."

Reggie Clifton drank deeply from his mug of beer, turning his head in doing so. From over the rim, his eyes focused on the person sitting at the bar. A small man, slight of build. Clifton burned into his mind every feature of his form and face. Reggie would need to keep a safe distance behind, and in case he had momentarily lost sight, he would still be able to find this accomplice in the crowded streets. "Holmes, what about these borrowed lamps at our feet. I feel honor bound to return them.

And what means of transportation will you and the Doctor use? I want to be prepared."

Sherlock smiled at Clifton's forethought in planning. "We will make it easy for our shadow to follow us. Dr. Collinsworth and I shall take an omnibus to the hotel. I would assume he would ride on top keeping himself hidden. You can follow in a hansom. There are so many on the street at this time of day that there would be no way for him to see that you had him in your sites.

Once the meal was complete, Reggie Clifton suddenly stood up and thundered, "Really Mr. Holmes, I've about had it with just sitting here doing nothing. I'm not waiting until the morrow to find the next clue. I am going to the Tower and disappear into the shadows, then when Anthony shows up, I'm going to ring his neck until he discloses where he is keeping Fiona Wilcox. Then after that, I will decide if I'm going to put a bullet into his brain and be rid of him forever." Reggie tipped over his chair for effect and stormed out of the pub.

As expected the man at the bar listened without giving himself away, but remained in his seat. Dr. Collinsworth paid the bill. Then he and Sherlock went out the door and waited for the omnibus going in their direction to arrive. A few minutes later their shadow came out the door and stood with his back to them, just one more man on the street waiting to catch a ride. When the omnibus did arrive, Holmes and Collinsworth climbed on board in the lower section. Their shadow, as Holmes assumed, went up top.

Chapter 23

Sherlock Holmes and Dr. Collinsworth sat in the Doctor's suite waiting for Reggie's return. It had been nearly seven hours since they parted company with Reggie Clifton. "Holmes, I'm getting worried that Reggie has been gone for such a long time. Do you think he is okay? I would feel just as bad if harm came to him as I would Fiona. This is all my fault. I should have never agreed to this whole setup with the royal family. If anything happens to either one, I'll…" He paused, "I don't know what I'll do."

At that moment the Doctor's angst was relieved by a knock on the door. Reggie Clifton entered with an exhausted countenance on his face. He came and sat with the two men, his head thrown back against the sofa. The Doctor excused himself briefly and returned with a covered tray setting it on the table in front of the couch. "I thought you might be hungry."

"Why thank you, Doctor." Reggie lifted the cover off the tray and found it loaded with roast beef sandwiches, deviled eggs and asparagus tips cooked in brandy sauce. "Doctor, there is enough here to feed a platoon. Won't you and Mr. Holmes join me?" But he didn't wait for an answer. He grabbed a sandwich and dug in.

By his second bite, the Doctor also retrieved a pewter stein with one of those hinged lids. "Here is something to wash that down with."

Reggie lustfully drank a large swallow wiping his face afterward with his soiled sleeve. "My God that hits the spot." He finished it off on the second pull.

Just as Reggie managed to stuff an entire deviled egg into his mouth, Holmes inquired, "Well Clifton, after following our shadow, do you have any information that might shed light on our situation?"

Reggie spoke with his mouth full, "I do," though it sounded more like oy-du. Reggie poured a glass of water and sluiced down the remains. "I'm sorry, yes I do. However, I'm not sure what to make of it. So I will start from the beginning. I followed you in a hansom from the pub. You were right that he would jump on the omnibus and be seated on the top deck. When you and the Doctor got to the corner nearest the hotel and debarked, he got off a block further down the street. I halted the cab and waited to see his next move. He doubled back staying a half block back from you, then he crossed the street. When he saw which hotel you two were about to enter, he posted himself at an outdoor cafe and nursed a pint for nearly two hours. I assume he was staking you out to see if you were going back out and would mimic your moves if you did so. My driver was more than willing to be at my service. He tended to his carriage and brushed his horse so that we did not stand out conspicuously.

After our mystery man was sure that you and Dr. Collinsworth were settled for the evening, he left on foot going South down Albermarle. I hung back having the coach stroll at a walking pace so that he was always in front of me. Then the man turned East on Piccadilly and hailed a hansom going his way. We kept a safe distance, and I never saw him even look back to see if he, in turn, was being followed. Can you guess where he finally ended up Mr. Holmes?"

Sherlock looked at him with the utmost confidence, "The Palace Theater."

"Yes. Just as you said earlier, that would be where we'll find Anthony Colton. Don't you think we should make our move now and catch him by surprise?"

"I will give you my answer after you finish with the details. There is more to your story, yes?"

"Well, what I saw was that he used a key to enter through the stage entrance. Then shortly, more people began appearing on the site. I counted seventeen men and women go through those doors. I made mental notes as to their size and shape, trying to capture each face in my mind so later when they came out I could account for them. A few hours later, they began to exit in two's and three's until all were gone. I felt I could identify each of them, and was sure that our man had not slipped through in the crowd. I was extra careful Mr. Holmes after what you told me about Anthony's disguises. I am sure Anthony Colton was not one of those who departed either. I waited an additional hour before another person left the building. A female, slender, and with blonde curls, wearing a wool hooded cloak, exited. I thought it must have been someone who had been there before I arrived. It did not occur to me at the moment, but she quickly moved into the shadows and was down the street before it dawned on me just how much she fit the general height and shape of our accomplice. I think I should have followed her Mr. Holmes, I'm sorry."

"Clifton, you have no reason to apologize. You did well, and your military training has proven exceptional. We now have confirmed that the theater is one of his locations. Whether he was there at this moment or not is not relevant. In answer to your earlier question about trying to surprise him there, Anthony Colton would not have Miss Wilcox in a location with so many comings and goings. He has her somewhere else at this time, but this also tells me that in his twisted patterns, he intends this to be where Miss Wilcox will be when the final act is finally played out.

Though it was after the fact, you were right that the blonde woman was the accomplice. She is the one who has given Colton access to the theater by the fact that she is in the cast for the upcoming play. We now have a distinct advantage and must press it to a satisfactory conclusion. Tomorrow, Clifton and I will allow ourselves to dangle on Colton's line for the time being. We will go to the Tower of London and look for the next clue. This is so that Anthony Colton does not suspect our knowing of the Theater. Meanwhile, Dr. Collinsworth, I have a special job for you. I am about to leave for a short time and will return with the props we will need."

"Anything you want Holmes, I would be most willing to do. So far, I feel like an anchor dragging bottom holding you back from catching Anthony Colton. And I'm truly sorry for how I complained in the tunnels. I'll try to be a better sport about it if only you'll give me another chance to prove myself."

Sherlock clasped the Doctor on the shoulder, "Yes, I was sure you would be willing to do as asked. Then let me tell you what I require. I want you to stake out the Palace Theater. If you see the woman, either as herself, or dressed as a man, or even Colton, I do not want you to do anything but observe."

"But won't they spot me? She has seen me up close and Anthony, of course, couldn't miss me even if he tried. I'm afraid I would not do justice with lurking in the shadows."

Sherlock's eyes danced, "Believe me, Doctor, by the time I'm through with you, your own mother wouldn't know who you are." Sherlock Holmes stood up, stretched his arms over his head and said, "Gentlemen, I suggest we all get a good night's sleep. Tomorrow could be another very long day." With that Holmes left the hotel room to complete his errands and allow the others to retire for the night.

Chapter 24

Long before daybreak, Sherlock was knocking on Dr. Collinsworth's door. It took several minutes before the Doctor climbed out of his warm bed, and attend to the bothersome knock When he opened the door, Holmes entered with a large bundle in his arms. "Sherlock, so early?"

"I need you in position before Clifton, and I leave for the Tower. Now if you would be so kind as to slip into these clothes. I think they should be a close enough fit for our purposes. Then I can finish my work on you."

In short order, Sherlock had Dr. Collinsworth made up and ready. They left the Doctor's room and went across the hall to Reggie Clifton's door. Holmes stood just out of site while Collinsworth tapped gently to gain entrance. Reggie answered the knock and momentarily was speechless, "Is that, you Doctor?" Collinsworth smile with bright white teeth was the only clue as to the identification of the man that stood before him.

Sherlock stepped into view saying, "I think this will be quite adequate for our needs."

"My compliments Mr. Holmes. I could have walked right by him and never given it a second thought," Reggie scratched his head in amazement.

"Good, then let us be off." Holmes threw a cloak over Dr. Collinsworth's shoulder, and the three men made their way down to the lobby. They were careful not to let the staff catch site of the Doctor. The less seen, the better. It would have been inconvenient to explain his attire, but fortunately, at this hour it was only the desk clerk that might have seen him. Reggie went over to the reception counter and distracted him from view while the Doctor and Holmes went through the front door.

It took some time to hail a cab at this hour. The driver gave them an odd look at seeing two well-dressed men and an apparent beggar but remained quiet thinking, men of wealth do strange things sometimes, but what business was it of his what they do. Holmes gave the directions to the driver, and they set off into the early dawn. As the driver reached Cambridge Circus, Holmes and Reggie Clifton deposited their charge a few blocks from the Palace Theater and left him to his task minus the gentleman's cloak.

The first light cast its arms of penetrating glow through the leaden clouds sharpening the silhouettes of the surrounding buildings. A lone figure made his way slowly down the street tapping the walkway with his walking stick. Dr. Collinsworth played his character of a blind man well to a very limited audience of early morning workers. He stopped short of walking into a crate jutting out having touched it with his cane. Collinsworth stepped to the side and continued on, feeling he had given a good show. Then moved to a location that gave him a full view of the theater but was out of the way of the soon to be pedestrians passing. He took out an empty cigar box from his coat and laid the prop next to his knee.

As the city began to stir, and residents started their day, witnessing one more unfortunate, begging along the avenue. Those who had compassion dropped a few coins in his box. Most, however, passed as if he were invisible, and a bobby or two gave a quick glance his way. The military ribbons Holmes had attached to his overcoat helped to give him certain allowances. Left on his own, Dr. Collinsworth kept a sharp eye through the dark glasses at the stage door of the theater.

Sherlock Holmes and Reggie Clifton had arrived near the gates of the Tower of London. Workmen and carts were moving through the gates eliminating that potential obstruction. "So Mr. Holmes, any idea where to start?"

"We shall go to the White Tower," Sherlock said with complete confidence.

"Why there?"

"The Limerick's lines, "Now that you have creep, it's time for you to sleep, you found your way, it's been a busy day, and tomorrow will be the keep.," tells us to go to the keep. That was a direct instruction. However, the preceding lines have additional instructions also. We had to creep in the tunnels; therefore, we need to seek out a similar entrance into the White Tower. Once there, it should lead us to what was once was the royal bedchambers.

Holmes and Clifton walked through the gates and strolled the grounds like tourists. Even at this early hour, others were also finding their way onto the grounds. The groundskeepers and staff were used to this daily occurrence, so when Sherlock came up to a stooped older man pushing a broad broom along the path. Holmes greeted him, "Good morning sir, "When do the doors open to the buildings?"

The old man took out a handkerchief to wipe his brow. "Oh, we never do lock the doors, never had a need to. Of course, there are exceptions, but those places are off limits to the public and very well guarded. But for the rest, there's not that much that one could walk away with. And if you did, eyes are watching everywhere, if you get my drift." The elderly man then continued with his chore of sweeping the walkway in his slow and methodical pace, leaving Holmes and Clifton to find their way.

Just before the two men were about to enter the building, Holmes spoke quietly, "We are being watched. Look just to your right, it's the cloaked woman now with her back to us."

Reggie moved his head slowly and just enough to see her. "Yes, that is the same cloak I saw last night and looks about the right size to me. Holmes, I could easily sprint and catch her off guard."

"A good thought, but for now let us proceed as planned. However, your suggestion has good merit, and I have an idea that would take any risk out of her fleeing from our grasp."

"Okay Holmes, then lead on. You have been right thus far, and I say, in for a penny, in for a pound."

They entered through the door and found they were at this moment the only ones inside the entry. Though there was no one to hear, Reggie whispered, "Where do we go from here Holmes?"

"This way." Sherlock led him towards the southeast corner of the tower. There, on the left side of the interior wall was an alcove, stark by design and mostly unadorned. Holmes scanned the room for a few seconds, then began walking over to a wall with a single dense weave tapestry. A quick glance back towards the entry area, making sure they were unseen, he pulled on the edge of the tapestry to reveal a small oak door approximately forty-eight inches high. Reaching in, he turned the iron handle, and it opened inwardly without difficulty. Holmes bent forward and went through the door with Reggie in tow. Once the tapestry was back in place, and the door closed, they found themselves in total darkness. The chamber was tall enough to stand straight and with arms extended Reggie could touch both sides of the walls. "I must say, Holmes, this is a bit unnerving." The small space consumed his voice to a muted muffle. Sherlock did not answer, but Reggie could hear Holmes rustling with something in his pockets. Then out of the darkness, a scratch, a whiff of sulfur, and a brilliant light burst forth. Holmes was holding a long stick match that one uses to light the fire in a hearth. Reggie gave a relieved laugh saying, "I should have known you would be completely prepared for this since you already knew we would be back in some sort of tunnel. And grateful I am because I could not imagine fumbling around here in the dark."

Holmes took out two candles from his outer pocket and lit them handing one to Reggie. Ahead was a set of stairs leading upward. They ventured forward along the hidden passage. Their shadows specters in lock step with them. The stone steps rasped with each footfall, but the darkness swallowed the sound effortlessly. Reggie asked, "So if you knew this tunnel led to the royal bedchambers, why didn't we go directly there to start with?"

"Two reasons actually. One, I was uncertain if we were allowed in the room, and I was sure Anthony Colton would have left the message somewhere here in this tunnel just like he had yesterday."

"My God Holmes, I never thought of that. I was only trying to get through here without screaming. I didn't tell you yesterday that I'm not all that comfortable in small places. Maybe someday I'll explain why. I'm sorry, but I wasn't looking for any clues as we have come through. Could we have missed it back there somewhere?"

"No, I think it will be near the end of this passage, and it looks like we're about there." Holmes' candle lit the back wall as they climbed the last stairs.

At the top of the stairs was a small landing and the end of the tunnel. A companion door matched the one on the lower level. What they saw gave pause. A pitcher sat on a narrow stand, liquid shimmered in the dull light of Sherlock's candle Below it written in soot, was the next clue. Reggie stared at the pitcher then asked, "What's the reason for the pitcher Holmes?"

"Had we done what was convenient going directly to the bedchambers, and searched out the twin entrance, upon entering, this pitcher was rigged to spill and undo his clue. You have to understand his way of thinking. If we refuse to be his puppets on a string, then he won't allow us to continue. Go through the tunnel give us our reward."

"How did you know we would go from the alcove on the first floor?

"He anticipated my deductive reasoning. An escape passage from the royal chambers would need to end near a safe exit, and the alcove would provide cover nearest the door. That made it the most logical location."

"Okay, what does the Limerick mean?" Reggie was more than ready to leave this confined space as quickly as possible.

The time has come where I now wary

Wasn't our little game so scary

But it's time to face

The blood and lace

And now you shall feel my fury

Holmes audibly sighed, "It's a dead end, there are no more clues to follow. He does not intend to draw us into a trap."

"I don't understand Holmes, why this charade. Why lead us on a wild goose chase?"

"I made a mistake. I thought Anthony Colton was using Fiona Wilcox as bait to extract his revenge on me. He knew, whether I had my memory or not, I would follow his clues by my very nature. He was counting on them in fact. Colton wanted us out of the way so he could stage his final act. If he can't kill Jesus, then Mother Mary would be his substitute. He sees it as both a completion of his earlier crime spree and for us, a form of mental torture."

"How can you conclude that Holmes?" Reggie Clifton asked in a defeated voice.

In answer, Sherlock undid the trigger rigged to the pitcher, then lowered it to the ground pouring the contents out onto the stone pavers. A mix of water and blood flowed across the stones and drained into the crevasses. Left behind was a small necklace. Reggie gasped, "That's Fiona's necklace."

"Yes, I've seen it on her many times."

"I'm going to kill him, Holmes. I'm going to kill him with my bare hands. I'm going to watch the life drain out of his eyes and smile in his face, so that is the last thing he sees."

"Steady man, we are not finished yet." Sherlock pulled out a white handkerchief and picked up the necklace. He laid it in the middle and folded it safely inside. I promise you, I will replace this around her warm neck before we are through. But now, there is no time to waste."

Holmes set his candle down, taking hold of the handle on the small door, he turned it and pushed. At first, the door would not budge, so Reggie added his weight with his shoulder giving it a collective effort. As the door inched outward, a squeak scraped across the floor. An oak cabinet had been set in front of the door hiding it in plain sight. In rushed welcoming light and fresh air filled the space bringing life to a dead and stale place. Pushing out a foot or so, they squeezed through the opening and stood up while the two men beat the dust from their clothes. In the far corner of the room, a stunned couple stared with utter surprise not believing their eyes. Sherlock nodded his head and said, "A private V.I.P. tour, but I can't really recommend it."

The couple just stood there frozen in place, dumbfounded, and unable to respond as Reggie Clifton pushed back the oak cabinet. Then as they were about to leave the room, Reggie turned to them and parted with these words, "Have a pleasant day."

Chapter 25

Sherlock Holmes and Reggie Clifton returned to the entry on the main floor. "Clifton, I want you to hang back here while I go towards the gate. Either our observer will follow me, or she will wait to see if you exit. Either way, we will trap her between us and close in to take possession of her." With the plan implemented, Holmes stepped out the door and with a quick step headed towards the gate.

The woman saw Sherlock leave alone, and was confused as to why his partner was not with him. She had not anticipated a split and hesitated a few moments. However, her instructions were clear, she was to follow Sherlock Holmes wherever he went. So she waited until he had just about arrived at the wall before she started to follow him. Her error was that she failed to look back, but kept her eye only on Holmes. Reggie Clifton was upon her before she knew what was happening. A pair of strong hands took hold of her arms from behind. "Not a word, keep walking forward without any trouble, or I'll snap your neck like a twig," Reggie whispered in her ear.

Holmes witnessed the abduction. Then quickly made for the gate to hail a carriage. This was achieved without delay. He climbed in holding the door open as Reggie led the young woman to the step. Sherlock reached out and took her hand and drew her up into the cab with Reggie at her heel. As the door closed, the driver flicked his whip above the flank of the chestnut colored horse. The coach sped off without any notice of bystanders.

The air was filled with tension as the cab gently rocked. Both men watched the young woman while she sat there; finally, she removed the hood of her cloak revealing the golden crown of hair that Reggie had noticed the other night. Her gray eyes glared defiance, and her painted lips were pressed tightly together daring them to make her speak. If looks could kill, Clifton and Holmes would be slumped over in a pool of their own blood. Instead, Sherlock had a hint of a smile on his face as he leisurely took out his pipe and laboriously completed his ritual of preparing to smoke. He sat back into his seat taking several puffs while contemplating the ceiling. Reggie Clifton understood Holmes' tactic and kept a straight face, looking forward, not giving their prisoner a person to vent on. Sherlock was softening her up without a single word. The color in her cheeks rose with each passing moment. Her breath held in, resistant to display any acceptance of her situation. Finally, her breath expelled in a huff. She snarled, "I'll not give you any information."

Holmes had her. Now was the time to press in. "You're an actress, and quite good really. I must compliment Anthony Colton on his disguise work. He did wonders on making you appear as a male, but it was your acting that made it so believable."

She interrupted, "I don't know what you are talking about, and I don't know anyone by that name. You have kidnapped me, and I'm frightened by what will happen to me. Please, stop this coach and let me out before I scream bloody murder."

Holmes grew silent again and returned to his pipe for a few minutes, and looked out the carriage window. When he finished, he opened the window in the carriage door and tapped out the ash from the pipe bowl. As he returned it to the inner pocket of his jacket, he said to Reggie, "Did you know that you can identify the type of tobacco used by the ash. I have made a study of it over the years, and it has led to solving a few cases that might not have been otherwise."

The young woman was now completely on edge. Sherlock finally looked at her directly and gave her his full attention. "Two nights ago, you met Anthony Colton at the gates of the Wellington Institute during the early hours before dawn. He brought with him a woman named Fiona Wilcox at knife point, I would assume. Then you fled back here to London and have been holding her against her will. It was you who oiled the doors both in the tunnels under the city and at the White Tower. Your shoe print will bear witness as well. It was something I had been working on a few years ago. I will use the unique impression of your fingers to show the court your presence there. At this juncture, you would be convicted of kidnapping. However, Anthony Colton intends to kill Miss Wilcox, and that makes you an accomplice to murder. For that crime, you will hang from the Gallows." Holmes stopped at that point and watched her reaction.

Beads of perspiration formed on her brow. Her eyes narrowed and moved from side to side weighing the consequences, but she still remained silent. Reggie looked from her to Holmes, then back again, wondering what his next play was. Before anything else could take place, the carriage arrived at the hotel. Reggie said to the woman, "Again, we go inside quietly. If not, I will take pleasure in saving The Crown the expense of a trial."

The woman was visibly shaken by the facts stated. When Reggie Clifton stepped out of the coach and took her hand, it was cold and moist. She climbed out but looked pale and was about to faint. Reggie steadied her until Sherlock could exit the cab and pay the driver. Then the men took positions on either side of her and led her up the steps, through the lobby, and up the stairs. They walked down the corridor three abreast unobserved.

They took her to Dr. Collinsworth's suite and sat her on the sofa. Sherlock went to the counter and poured her a sherry. Returning, it was a shaking hand that received the glass. She sipped at the sherry while Reggie Clifton started to pace the room. "How much longer must we wait here, Mr. Holmes? I'm not going to stand by while Anthony does God only knows what to Fiona." He looked menacingly at the young woman, which made her all that more unsteady.

The answer came with the twist of a knob. All eyes turned to the entry door as Dr. Collinsworth came through still dressed in his beggar's attire. "Mr. Holmes, Reggie, I have news." He then noticed the young woman sitting on his sofa, looking rather nervous. "Who is this?", he asked as he started to shed his disguise.

Sherlock said, "This is the small man who followed us into the pub yesterday."

Dr. Collinsworth walked up to the woman for a closer look. "Remarkable! I would have never guessed. "He bent down lower to study her face, "Only the nose is the same, otherwise..." His voice dropped off as he stood erect.

"Very observant of you Doctor. Anthony Colton had no reason to make alterations to either her eyes or nose, never expecting us to discover her presence. But you have news for us," Holmes asked expectantly.

"First I need a Brandy, then we will get down to business." He poured himself a stiff drink and threw back half of it in a swig.

"Better. First, let me tell you just how difficult it can be getting through the lobby dressed like this. Not only did I have to show them my card, but they were suspicious until I displayed the near one-hundred pounds in my wallet. Even after that, I felt their eyes drilling into my back." The doctor was quite enjoying himself in the telling of his story. "Oh, and you should have seen the reaction from the legless veteran when I emptied the contents from my cigar box into his tray. Really, Holmes, one could make a decent living on a street corner if they lived frugally."

Sherlock interrupted, "Doctor, what did you see that has brought you back so quickly?"

The doctor took a deep breath, "Sorry, all this running around and spying has got me all lathered up. What I saw, was a dray cart that delivered a guillotine prop, though the blade certainly fooled me. It looked razor sharp and glistened in the sun reflecting off it. Then there was the man who came out to receive it. He looked nothing like Anthony, but there was just something in his movements that made me wonder for a moment. Well, that's it. That is what took place, and I thought maybe I should report back to you. What do you say, Mr. Holmes?"

"Dr. Collinsworth, again your keen observations do you credit, and, your timing is impeccable. What you observed will pay generous dividends in solving this crime. You have indeed confirmed Anthony Colton's presence at the Palace Theater, and the fact that he is there at this moment." Sherlock spoke this last sentence as he turned to the woman.

She froze in place, staring at him. Then buried her face in her hands, dropping the glass, and spilling the remaining contents onto the area rug. Through racks of tears, she confessed, "I love him. I always have loved him, ever since we were children and I first set eyes on him. From that day he has ruled my world."

As the floodgates opened, she told them she was Hillary Edwards, Daughter of Lord and Lady Edwards of Cheshire, and that she was a distant cousin to Anthony Colton. "We met when I was twelve years old and he sixteen. From the first day, he could talk me into anything he wanted. Mostly those things were fun and games, but every once in awhile he would play a prank on the servants that often ended in a reprimand to the staff. Later his father discovered Anthony's actions had been unbecoming to his position, so he sent him out of the country. At the time, he told me it was a military school, but later I learned that he had been sent to France to a private school. I did not believe the rumor that he had started mutilating animals and that was the reason for his being sent away." The tears had finally run their course, and she dried her eyes before continuing, "I lost contact with him after that. It was not until I received a letter from him that said he was back in London and wanted me to return to him. He didn't bother to ask if I had married or waited for his return, he just assumed so, and he was right. Much to my parents' angst, they could not understand my not marrying. They were surprised when I suddenly, out of the blue, said I wanted to go to London to take drama classes. Of course, my mother told me it was beneath my station to do something so common, but my father could never refuse me the slightest whim.

So, that fall I attended a small private academy and came to London with a governess She was neither bright nor curious. As long as I presented myself in public in a way that was befitting my position, she never questioned my coming or going, regardless of the hour. Anthony took me to a dilapidated warehouse, but once inside, he showed me the world I never knew he lived in. He would alter our appearance, and we would go out into society both high and low. All the while, no one ever knew our real identities.

There came a time when Anthony would become sullen on a given day, then very animated the next. It was during these times, he would dress me up and send me out on errands, or give me a name that I would make inquiries, then follow and report to him on their whereabouts. Anthony never explained the reasons, and I never asked.

Then six years ago, he again disappeared from my life. Leaving not a word nor letter to let me know what happened to him. That all changed nine months ago when I was handed a letter sent by him, from that Institute. He told me that he was soon to leave and I was to prepare his accommodations and gain access to the Palace Theater. All was prepared as instructed accordingly. I waited for his call to come. The days passed so slowly, and I grew faint of heart, wondering if I was ever really to see him. When word came, I appropriated the horse and carriage and arrived at the stated hour. Until the moment he came out with the woman, I had no knowledge of his plan. I was confused, Mr. Holmes. What was I to do? I've waited all these years never allowing another man into my life. Here he was, back in my life, we were together again, and that was what I wanted. I was afraid to ask why he had brought the other woman, and I didn't want to know. He just explained that she was part of a great injustice and would be released when it was made right." Hillary was spent emotionally.

Holmes took a seat next to her then asked, "Where is Anthony Colton keeping Miss Wilcox?"

"She is now in a small but comfortable room on the third floor of the theater. Anthony also moved there yesterday on the same floor." She took Holmes' hand into hers and with a pleading look said, "Please Mr. Holmes, don't harm him."

Sherlock withdrew his hand and stood up. "That will depend entirely on him. Dr. Collinsworth, I need you to stay with Miss Edwards while Clifton and I go to the Palace Theater. Clifton, bring your revolver."

With those words, Hillary Edwards broke down into tears again. The Doctor, being a kind man, gave what comfort he could.

Chapter 26

Sherlock Holmes made ready to leave, his hand on the doorknob, as Dr. Collinsworth looked up from his charge, "Sherlock, if at all possible… Can we leave out calling in a constable in this affair?"

Holmes immediately understood the bind Dr. Collinsworth was in. "In this case, the fewer, the better. Come Clifton."

A coach was hailed by the hotel doorman for the two gentlemen. Holmes instructed the driver, "Palace Theater and quickly." They climbed into the coach and sat across from each other.

The horseshoes clapping out their beat drowned out the hum of the city as the two men sat quietly in the cab. Sherlock took the opportunity to smoke his pipe again in an almost ritualistic manner, while Reggie's countenance took on the demeanor of a soldier silently preparing himself for battle. His eyes glazed over and he appeared as a statue. "What's our plan, Holmes? Do we wait for him to show his face, or do we force our way in?"

Sherlock puffed on his pipe a few times before looking Reggie in the eyes, "Let's assess the situation after we arrive. I think there will not be much if any, activity in or around the building. After which, we will take what measures are needed."

The coach driver deposited his fares just around the corner from the front of the theater. Holmes instructed him to wait for their return and be ready to go at a moment's notice. The stage door was across the street. Holmes viewed the building out the coach window looking for any windows facing that side. Were they blacked out? Yes. That allowed Holmes and Clifton to exit the carriage and walked directly to the stage door. When they got there, Sherlock took out a key from his vest pocket. He inserted it and turned the lock. "Holmes, where did you get that key?"

Sherlock stated calmly, "From the right-hand pocket of Miss Edwards' cloak. I saw her feel for it during her coach ride. She was thinking of how she might dispose of it before we searched her. So when I sat next to her, I lifted it as she finished her story."

The only sound was a light click of the lock. The door swung out without noise. Reggie shook his head, "You amaze me, Holmes. Now let's get that Bastard."

The hall was dimly lit but clear of obstruction. They moved forward as quietly as possible to the back stairs. Holmes was just about to start his ascent when Reggie could no longer contain himself. He pushed past Sherlock and bounded up the steps, two at a time. "Clifton, NO!" Holmes called out just above a whisper. But Reggie was not to be denied. Sherlock quickened his pace in an attempt to catch up with Reggie. However, Reggie Clifton disappeared through a red velvet drape covering the casing at the top of the stairs. Before Holmes got to the top of the landing, he heard a loud thud and Reggie calling out. Sherlock moved the curtain aside to reveal an open trap door in the middle of the hall floor. Looking down into it, Reggie lied on a crumpled pile of an area rug that had covered the trap door. It looked that this was used to move props from the backstage to storage on the upper level. "Clifton, I'll come back down and help you."

Reggie yelled back up to Holmes, "Sorry Holmes, I've broken my leg. You must go on without me."

"Are you sure Clifton? Sherlock called back.

"Yes Holmes, go… Go." Clifton's voice was louder than needed. Was it from the pain, or was there another reason for shouting out to go? But Holmes wasted no more time and left Reggie behind to fend for himself. At the end of the hall was the second set of stairs leading to the third floor. Holmes moved cautiously looking for any additional traps. He reached the top of the landing where there was a closed door. Sherlock took hold of the handle and turned it slowly, by increments he pushed open the door all the while searching for a trigger to spring a trap. Instead, there was only an empty hallway with two doors on opposite sides. One door was slightly ajar with a dim light showing through the cracks. Sherlock approached the closed door first and tried the knob, but it was locked. He then drew up alongside the wall just past the door opening and reached out giving a quick push to the door. It swung open and hit the interior wall with a thud. Peering in he saw a vacant room with three doors all on the same wall. A single bare bulb hanging from the ceiling illuminated the room, and a straight back chair stood in the corner near the window.

Holmes entered the room turning full circle. Nothing was in plain sight but had not looked behind the door yet. As he moved the door, there on the wall was another Limerick from Colton.

I really hate to be such a bore

But you must now choose a door

Choose wrong and she'll lose her head

And at your hands will be dead

Then that will be the end of this whore

Each of the doors had a peephole, so Sherlock took his time to view through each to see what he could gather. It was a single room lit by a candelabra with three candles burning. Shadows swayed across the walls from an apparent draft. The peepholes gave their limited view putting together a puzzle of the image within. But there at the center of the room, Fiona Wilcox lay firmly tied to a cot. Her head laid upon a satin pillow placed on a wood block. Fiona's necked stretched through a hole in a Guillotine and the blade positioned menacingly overhead.

Fiona's eyes were wide with fear having heard the door in the outer room slam against the wall only moments ago. Three cords were attached to the lever of the Guillotine. Perhaps all three doors would bring the same fate, but Holmes saw no other choice than to choose one of them.

He stepped back looking at the three doors racking his brain, seeking a clue as to which to choose. He boldly stepped up to the middle door, grabbed the handle and opened it stepping in quickly as he moved towards Fiona Wilcox. From a gagged mouth, she let out a muffled scream in response. Sherlock Holmes hurried to her side and began untying the ropes that bound her. Then he pulled her head free from the damnable contraption, while the blade remained in place.

Holmes was working on the cords that held her hands bound when Fiona let out another muted scream. Anthony Colton stood in the opening of the door that Sherlock had so recently passed through. A gun held in his right hand was pointing at Sherlock. "Hello Sherlock Holmes," Colton said with a sneer in his voice. "I must congratulate you on your choice of door. Just how did you manage to deduce the correct one?"

Holmes looked at Anthony Colton as if addressing an old friend, "Well, it came down to a simple solution. I guessed." Fiona's head swung suddenly to Holmes' face, eyes even wider, a small squeal escaped through the gag.

"Truly a pity Mr. Holmes. I was looking forward to the show, the anguish it would have brought you. I envisioned her head rolling to your feet and you standing there incapacitated with shock as I walked up behind you and put a bullet into your marvelous brain. It would have been the last thing you saw before leaving this world." The hatred glowed from Anthony Colton. "Well, I will have to alter the scenario a bit and shoot you first. Then put Miss Wilcox back on the cot and exit through one of the other doors. And by the way, I assume since my shadow has not returned, you must have caught her and now Dr. Collinsworth is holding her. It's a shame, she was to perform as Mary mother of Jesus at tonight's opening, and I had such a spectacular death planned for her. But now I'll have to deal with her in some other fashion fitting for the occasion."

Anthony Colton smiled with pleasure as he raised his pistol to take aim at Sherlock. "Now look into my eyes, Holmes. This shall be the last thing you see."

The loud explosion of gunfire reverberated off the walls of the room. Anthony Colton spun as if struck by a sledge hammer. The gun in his hand flew across the room landing at Sherlock's feet. Anthony's arm bloomed a crimson red as a hand grabbed him by his jacket collar and pushed him up against the wall.

Anthony turned his head, confused at first. Then realization set in, Reggie Clifton had a firm hold on him. He stammered a single word, "But...?"

Chapter 27

The coaches traversed the city streets like so many others. The train station their final destination. Inside the lead coach was Reggie Clifton with Anthony Colton beside him. Reggie's revolver was poking in the ribs of Colton making sure he did not try some scheme to escape. "I have paid the driver generously for his silence, and he will wait with us until the train is about to depart." Reggie Clifton sat erect, a look of self-confidence having completed a successful mission. Whereas, Anthony sat dejected and morose.

In the other carriage was Dr. Collinsworth, Fiona Wilcox, and Sherlock Holmes. Their carriage drew up to the platform, and they debarked and headed for their private berth on the train. Their wait would still be near an hour before departure. Once inside and seated, Fiona's head found the comfort of Dr. Collinsworth's shoulder and quickly she began to slumber. The last few days had been a nightmare for her, and only now did she feel safe enough to relax. Sherlock sat across from them and put his feet up on the cushion next to the doctor. Collinsworth spoke softly asking Sherlock, "I'm still trying to understand how this all washed out Holmes."

"Quite simple really," said Holmes. "When Clifton had fallen in through the trap door, he immediately saw an opportunity for deception. I knew the moment he shouted out that he had broken his leg, that it was a ruse."

Reggie came in through the sliding door at that very moment and having heard what Holmes was saying he added, "I waited until Holmes went up the third flight of stairs. I half expected Anthony's face to have appeared over the edge of the trap door and try to eliminate me while lying on the floor. But when he did not show up, I managed to find my way back to the original stairs and climbed them stealthily this time. Once I was on the third floor, I waited in the shadows of the landing until I saw Anthony pass through the door from across the hall into the room Mr. Holmes had entered a few minutes before. Arrogance was Colton's downfall. I had outflanked him, and he never suspected my pretense. I moved closer and overheard the conversation. Then seeing him raise his arm to shoot, I did what was necessary and fired first, aiming to disarm him."

Sherlock took out his pipe examining it, then put it back in his pocket changing his mind. "How ironic, Anthony Colton was, disarmed in the same manner, those many years ago."

Dr. Collinsworth started to look puzzled, realizing, "Reggie, where is Anthony?"

"Don't worry Doctor. I have him safely bound and gagged. And just for insurance, I gave him a shot of Laudanum, so he isn't feeling any pain and will most likely sleep until we arrive at our destination."

The expression of relief on the doctor's face came quickly. "Gentlemen, I don't know how to thank you both for bringing this affair to such a welcome conclusion." All three sets of eyes drifted to the sleeping Fiona Wilcox.

Sherlock leaned deeper into his seat, closed his eyes and said, "To quote William Shakespeare, 'all's well that ends well.'"

****

When they arrived at the gate of the Wellington Institute, the sky had turned dark and foreboding weighing heavily on Sherlock Holmes. He put the feelings aside for the time being and helped Dr. Collinsworth get Fiona Wilcox back into the building without being seen. They took her to one of the guest suites and helped her get settled. "Would you like a sedative my dear? It would help you sleep." The Doctor fawned over her.

"Thank you, but I'm really fine. Surprisingly, Anthony did not treat me poorly during my time with him. That is until he tied me up and stuck me under that Guillotine. Then, I was a little bit concerned. After all, I'm very much attached to my head."

Dr. Collinsworth looked stunned for a moment, then laughed until he had tears in his eyes. "Oh my dear, only you could go through something like this and make a joke about it. Have I told you lately just how incredible a woman you are?" The Doctor threw his arms around her, "Okay, if you need anything, Please let me know. I'll have dinner sent up this evening, and we can meet first thing in the morning."

Holmes was standing near the door as the doctor and Fiona hugged. Fiona gazed his way and said, "Thank you, Mr. Holmes, I'm sure we will see each other soon. Please get some rest, I'm sure you are worn out by this little adventure." Her smile was radiant and conveyed all he needed from her.

Dr. Collinsworth and Holmes left her room when the Doctor said, "I made sure Reggie held Anthony at the station for a couple of hours. I did not want Fiona to have to deal with seeing him being brought back here to the Institute. After Reggie gets Anthony settled, I'm hoping the three of us can sit down to dinner this evening and talk. Well, and yes, celebrate too. So please join us around eight o'clock, yes?"

"As you wish. I think we have much to talk about," Holmes sounded a bit defeated.

Sherlock returned to his room. Entering, he felt how strange it was that he had spent so much time here, and now he saw it as a place that felt foreign like he did not belong here any longer. His memory coming back created a new problem. Just how was he going to deal with it? Perhaps he was tired and not thinking straight. A good meal and a good night sleep should help clear his head. First things first, he bathed and put on a fresh suit. It was almost eight o'clock, so he went downstairs to join the good Doctor and Clifton.

When Sherlock got to the dining room, he saw Clifton and Dr. Collinsworth sitting at the far corner table. Was it because Sherlock almost always sat at that table, or was Dr. Collinsworth a creature of habit like himself? The Doctor spotted Holmes and started to wave enthusiastically to him. As Holmes approached, Collinsworth said, "Let me buy you a drink." Then he chuckled at his own joke.

It appeared to Sherlock that the doctor had already had a few drinks to start with. But Holmes would give allowances under the circumstances. Sherlock sat heavily into his seat. Then placed his hands folded on the table. His body language conveyed what words did not.

Dr. Collinsworth quickly became aware of the change in Sherlock Holmes. "Mr. Holmes, I can never repay you for what you did, and you have my deepest gratitude. However, I can clearly see that something is troubling you. Let us not speak about it tonight, for this should be a time for celebration, but please come to my office first thing tomorrow, say, ten o'clock. I have a feeling that any earlier, I would not be of any use to you." The Doctor grinned as he held up his drink.

Sherlock nodded his head in acknowledgment, "Okay Doctor, I will look forward to speaking with you then." Holmes paused a moment before asking, "Dr. Collinsworth, Miss Wilcox went through a nightmare that no woman should have to ever experience. She seemed to be holding up, but is she really able to put this behind her?"

"Why Mr. Holmes, thank you for your compassion toward her. Yes, she is a woman with a solid character and a heart of a lion. I depend on her probably more than I should, but she has shown herself more than capable. I will watch her for any signs of trauma over the next week or so. But for now, let us raise our glasses to toast Fiona." Collinsworth lifted his glass and said, "To the most incredible woman that any of us will ever meet." The Doctor drained his glass and gave Holmes and Clifton a hardy grin.

Then Sherlock changed the subject, "And what do you plan to do with Anthony Colton?"

Dr. Collinsworth slowly shook his head, "It was most unfortunate, we learned our lesson the hard way, but rest assured, Anthony Colton will not be creating a scene anytime soon."

Then Reggie voiced, "If you would like, I will take you to Anthony's new quarters after dinner. I think you will find the accommodations befitting his current status at this institution." Reggie had a satisfied glint in his eyes and Holmes could tell Reggie Clifton was going to take pleasure in what he had to show him. "Tell me, Mr. Holmes, I'm a bit curious as to why you let Hillary Edwards go. After all, she was at least guilty of kidnapping?"

"Miss Edwards was a foolish young woman. However, I believed her when she said that she had no knowledge that Colton had intended to kidnap Miss Wilcox. I also think he would have dealt severely with her if she had refused to be his accomplice. Under the circumstances, it would not serve justice to have turned her over to the police."

Dr. Collinsworth speech was now slurred when he said, "I concur, Mr. Holmes, it would have been most difficult to have to explain ourselves to the authorities. No, as you said earlier on the train,"All's well that ends well." Miss Wilcox will recover quickly, and Anthony has burned his bridges as far as I'm concerned."

The doctor drained his glass then signaled for another to go with his dinner. Though he was in a celebratory mood, the other two men were quiet and solemn, so soon, the party fizzled into silence. It was not until dinner had concluded that Dr. Collinsworth brought out from under the table an inlaid box made from exotic woods from the Far East, and handed it to Holmes. "Perhaps you would like to try one of these now that dinner is finished. They are Cuban cigars. I have a friend who lives in Havana, and he sends me a box every Christmas, along with a case of rum. I have been saving these for a special occasion, and this most definitely qualifies as such. Please accept this with my greatest gratitude."

"Thank you, Doctor." Sherlock opened the box and offered a cigar to Clifton, who shook his head, then to Collinsworth, who was happy to accept.

The Doctor said, "I could run upstairs and retrieve a bottle of rum to go with this if you would like. There is nothing better after dinner than to light up one of these and sip Cuban rum."

Holmes responded, "Thank you, but this will be just fine as is." He lit the cigar and let the rich flavor hover in his palette.

The men grew quiet again. A blue-grey cloud enveloped them as they sat back in their chairs puffing away. When they had finished, Reggie asked, "Mr. Holmes, are you ready to see Anthony's new accommodations?"

Sherlock stood up. "I will see you in the morning Doctor," then turned to Reggie, "lead the way, Clifton."

Reggie led Holmes down a set of stairs into the basement. Then along a dimly lit brick-walled corridor to the end. There, a single steel door stood alone. Reggie walked up to it and slid a three-inch by eight-inch metal plate slotted in the door to one side. "Take a look for yourself, Mr. Holmes."

Inside was a ten foot by ten-foot brick walled cell, a single cot, and a straight back wood chair. Anthony Colton sat with his back to the door and did not flinch when the slide was moved. The only light came from a small window with an iron grate twelve feet above the floor.

Holmes stepped back, and Reggie closed the opening. "There Mr. Holmes is where Anthony Colton will spend his remaining days, and it could not have happened to a nicer guy. Have a good evening sir." Reggie Clifton walked away with a grand smile on his face.

Chapter 28

The next morning Sherlock Holmes went straight to Dr. Collinsworth's office. "Good morning Mr. Holmes. Did you rest well?"

"No, not particularly Doctor."

"I'm sorry to hear that, won't you please join me on the sofa. I have tea and scones fresh from the kitchen, and they're still warm." The Doctor set a tray on the end table.

Sitting down with Dr. Collinsworth was a common occurrence, but now it felt bizarre. Sherlock was not the same man that he was a few days ago, and now would never be. The Doctor poured the tea as Sherlock liked it, milk first, then topped off with the earl grey. Handing the cup to him, Sherlock thanked him in a quiet voice, "Thank you."

"Sherlock." Dr. Collinsworth smiled warmly at him. "I feel after all that we have been through together over these last few days, I consider you my friend. And so using your first name seems appropriate. Agreed?" Sherlock nodded his head twice.

"I'm a pretty good detective in my own right. I see into the minds of others and pick up on the clues the body gives evidence to, so bear with me a moment. How long has it been since you parted company with Dr. Watson?"

"Watson?" Holmes exclaimed.

"Yes, that was the only name you gave me with your memory loss." The Doctor knew Sherlock did not remember his being at the Institute.

Holmes did the math, "A shade over two and a half years."

"And where was that?" the Doctor asked

"I sent him back to the village of Meiringen."

Dr. Collinsworth asked, "What happened there, Sherlock?"

"Dr. Watson and I were pursuing Professor Moriarty."

"But?" The doctor was now leaning in towards Holmes.

Holmes considered all the therapy over the last year, "But, there is no Professor Moriarty."

Dr. Collinsworth's eyes conveyed great compassion, but he did not withhold the punches. "Who was he to you?"

Sherlock's voice became stronger, "He was my mirror image, my alter ego. I needed someone who was a true challenge to me."

"So you created your own arch-enemy." Holmes silently nodded his head. "So what took place?"

"I faked my death." Dr. Collinsworth remained still as Sherlock took a sip of his tea. Holmes just stared at his cup.

"Why Sherlock? Why fake your death?" The Doctor asked quietly.

Sherlock Holmes turned to face Dr. Collinsworth, "Because, I could not do it anymore. There was no challenge to any of it. I was using Cocaine more and more and then slip into periods of just sitting in my chair and staring at the fire in the fireplace. Watson would sit at his desk and write of our adventures, asking for a detail here and there. I may have been hooked on Cocaine, but Dr. Watson was hooked on the adrenaline of the hunt." Holmes felt more exposed than he had ever felt before.

"So what now Sherlock?" the Doctor asked in a steady voice.

"I don't know." Holmes snapped at the Doctor.

"Do you want to go back? Back to the life, you led before?"

"Yes. But I can't." A sulk crept into his voice.

Dr. Collinsworth chuckled, "I'm sorry Sherlock, as your friend, not your doctor, I must say you have an incredible ego." Holmes looked startled as the Doctor continued, "you can't because you would have to admit that you have frailties and faults like the rest of us?"

Holmes sighed, "How could I face Watson or members of Scotland Yard, for that matter, with the fact that I've lost three years of my life that I can't account for. I could lie, but I find that repugnant."

The Doctor asked kindly, "My friend if you could go back to your previous life without these last three years, would you?"

"How could that even be possible? I can't change what has been."

Dr. Collinsworth smiled, "Some of it was already done."

Holmes went from startled to being shocked. "What do you mean?"

"In the first month or so, we found Dr. Watson, and he came here to the Institute. It was from him we learned of Professor Moriarty. It was the low point, but also the beginning of your recovery. When you could not face issues with Moriarty, you went catatonic, and it was necessary to wipe the slate clean so that you had no memory of Dr. Watson's coming here."

Sherlock searched his memory. "How is it possible that I have no memory of his being here?"

"It's possible because you wanted it to be. So again I ask, do you want to go back to London as if these three years never were?"

Holmes considered all the avenues before responding, "Yes."

"Fine. By the time we are finished, your life will begin anew the moment Reggie Clifton drops you off on the streets of London. There will be no memory of any of us here, and instead, I will replace a new memory of this time and where you have been. This will take work and won't happen overnight, but we'll get there, and you can be the man you have always been."

****

Sherlock Holmes left Dr. Collinsworth's office and found himself going back out into the gardens, walking the pebbled paths deep in thought.

The idea of altering his history troubled him. He felt it was a betrayal to himself, dishonest somehow, but the alternative was even worse. He could never face his old friend Watson again, even though Watson knew his condition, and he would never be able to take on another case after this. Those at Scotland Yard would suspect even if they failed to find out the details, and

Holmes would see it on their faces no matter what. So, he could retire, he had the means. He could lead a comfortable but quiet life. No, he thought, he might as well put a gun to my head.

Sherlock was shaken loose from his thoughts when he saw Fiona Wilcox sitting on the bench in the middle of the rose garden. He noticed though her hair was close-cropped, it somehow was styled into a very feminine style. As he approached, her hands that were laying in her lap, rose at his presence and started to fuss with her hair. "I look dreadful." Her fingers combed through the short locks.

"Quite the contrary I must say. I think I have never seen you more beautiful than here at this moment sitting among the roses, a Greek Goddess."

She began to giggle, "Mr. Holmes, you are too much." But the smile on her lips and within her eyes said it was just what she needed at this very moment.

"May I sit down with you?" Holmes asked

"Please." She scooted over a bit and adjusted her dress smoothing it out with the palms of her hands. He sat beside her and remained quiet for a minute while viewing the grounds, and he could hear her deep breathing.

He broke the silence, "You went through a horrible experience, Miss Wilcox. I wish I had been able to get to you earlier. No one should have had to go through what you did, I'm so sorry."

She took his hands in hers and looked up into his eyes, "Dr. Collinsworth told me all that you did for me last night. He said you were quite remarkable in the pursuit of Anthony Colton and it was a miracle that you were able to save my life, for which I'm incredibly grateful," She surprised Sherlock by kissing him on the cheek. "He also told me about his plans to give you an altered memory."

Holmes asked, "Does he tell you everything?"

Her eyes grew bright, "Why yes Sherlock, he does, and I'm guessing you are having trouble with it."

"I can see why Dr. Collinsworth confers with you. You really do have a brilliant mind. I think he is right in trying to influence you to pursue a doctorate."

"Thank you for the vote of confidence, but I'm quite happy with my work here at the Institute. Besides, quite frankly, I'm not sure how Dr. Collinsworth could get along without me." She said this with a knowing smile. "Sherlock," she turned serious, "forget all the reasons you're thinking of not allowing Dr. Collinsworth to do his work with you. I feel I know you pretty well after the last couple years, and I know you could never be happy with yourself in this present state."

Sherlock interrupted, "Who said I was ever happy?"

Fiona gave him a half grin. "You know what I mean. You could never live with yourself, I'm only sorry that you will no longer remember me." She nodded her head slightly, "Yes, I have grown quite fond of you and your charming ways Mr. Holmes. But it is time for you to go back home where you belong and do what you are good at." She stood up, then turned to Sherlock bending at the waist. She kissed Sherlock Holmes on the lips, "Goodbye Mr. Holmes." Then she walked away.

Chapter 29

A letter arrived at the home of Dr. John Watson.

My Dear John,

I have fantastic news for you. Ever so recently Sherlock Holmes has recovered his memory in full. There was a near-disastrous event involving one of our patients and Miss Wilcox. However, in making my decision to bring Mr. Holmes into my confidence, it was by happy accident that the very circumstances were what triggered his memory. In an instant, he had full facility and recall. He single-handedly dealt with a problem so far beyond my capabilities to handle. As I was later to learn, you and Mr. Holmes had had dealings with this patient years earlier. Does Anthony Colton ring a bell? Please keep this in complete confidence, Colton has a great deal to do with this facility and would cost us dearly if this event were to be made public.

Further, suffice it to say Sherlock Holmes is recovered from the issues that brought him here in the first place. You will need to trust me that I can not reveal those issues. It could compromise what I'm about to do. There is a caveat that we must discuss. As we did in the past when your coming here had so affected his well-being, Mr. Holmes has agreed that it would be better as if these last few years had never happened.

So, I need your assistance to make this possible. First, I will leave it to you to explain to Sherlock's brother Mycroft, in whatever way you deem necessary, that he was the one who kept safe the home on Baker Street and not you in reality. I would assume you have already told Mycroft that Sherlock was alive. The reason for this deception is that when Sherlock has his new memory, he will believe he was in control from the very beginning and Mycroft was his contact during his absence.

Second, and this will be much more challenging, you will be required to suppress all that has taken place and act as if whatever Sherlock tells you is what actually happened over these lost years. Can you do this John? I will keep you up to date as we progress to its final conclusion. Until then, I look forward to hearing from you soon.

Ever your friend,

Reginald

Dear Reginald,

I can't tell you how relieved I am, hearing from you concerning Holmes. It truly is a miracle how he has recovered. Needless to say, yes, I would do anything to have my friend back. Please let me know what that entails, and I'll be the best actor you will ever come across.

At the time, I thought it best to allow everyone to believe that Sherlock Holmes had met his demise including his brother Mycroft. After all our discussions, I hoped that a solution would arise that would solve the issue. You can only imagine how shocked and relieved Mycroft was when I informed him that Sherlock was alive and well. I did, however, withhold most of the information telling him it was important to not know of his circumstances. He too is most willing to do as asked and will never bring up the question to Sherlock. Do you have an idea how long before Holmes returns to us? Thank you again for all you are doing to bring him back home.

I'm ever in your debt,

John

John,

I would have loved to have asked Sherlock for suggestions as to what took place during these years. However, it was necessary that they were new thoughts, for I did not want any possible link in his memory that might undo what is taking place.

That being said, I must apologize in advance. I have tried to be creative and think as Sherlock Holmes would. But I'm just a country doctor and am doing my best to be believable. It is impossible to implant details over such a long time span. So, I am giving him impressions that he, himself, will fill in and will be quickly put into the past. In fact, I'm counting on it. I hope Sherlock has never been to Tibet. I don't want conflicting memories to confuse the matter. Why Tibet you may ask, well it was about as far away from here as one could get, and a very long time to do so. Besides, I did spend several years in India and had always hoped that I could have gone to see those majestic mountains. In this way, I feel as if I'm leaving a small part of me with a person I now consider a good friend.

I shall not tell you the exact day of his arrival, it should be a genuine surprise on your part, and I don't want to make it any more difficult than it already will be. So this my friend is goodbye. I trust you will destroy our correspondence and if ever we meet again, maybe we can renew our friendship again.

Yours Truly,

Dr. Reginald Collinsworth

****

It was early April, and the weather continued to be true to form. Variant shades of grey dominated the sky. Rain, came off and on while the train to London moved with its passengers. Holmes and Reggie Clifton sat most of the trip quietly. Then debarked on a crowded platform to a waiting carriage. The streets seemed not to notice their presence, and they made quick progress to their destination. Dusk was nearly at hand as the carriage pulled up to the curb.

"Well Mr. Holmes, this is my goodbye." Reggie extended his hand, and as they shook, Reggie said the trigger phrase, "The time has come to part." Wordlessly Sherlock exited the cab and looked down the street. Reggie Clifton knocked on the ceiling signaling the driver to leave.

Sherlock Holmes blinked a few times and thought to himself how could I have walked down this street and been unaware of doing so. It was time for him to return to Watson and resume his life as it was before. He strolled away feeling refreshed, and maybe happy for the first time in his life.

From across the street, a black hansom with curtains held a red-headed woman who watched as Sherlock Holmes walked briskly away.

To the reader: Sir Arthur Conan Doyle, killed off Sherlock Holmes in, "The Memoirs of Sherlock Holmes". Then a few years later he brought Holmes back in, "The return of Sherlock Holmes".

I have always thought that a better explanation for Sherlock Holmes was needed as to what really happened during those missing years. It is my hope that this story does just that, and fits with Doyle's character with added humanity.

If you enjoyed this book, please give it a review and pass it on to others. Thank you, Don Henwood

Made in the USA
Middletown, DE
19 October 2017